The Muddy Road to Glory

THE MUDDY ROAD
TO GLORY

☆

Stephen W. Meader

ILLUSTRATED BY GEORGE HUGHES

ISBN 978-1-931177-54-2 cloth
ISBN 978-1-931177- 55-9 paperback

Library of Congress Catalog Card Number 63-17005

SOUTHERN SKIES

LITTLE ROCK, ARKANSAS

www.southernskies.com

Dedication

The republication of this book is dedicated to Dave Atkins by his friend and partner, Jerry Atchley.

The Muddy Road To Glory

Foreword

In this story I have tried to picture the everyday life of a young Union soldier in the Civil War; his adventures, his sufferings, and his growth from a callow boy to full manhood.

Ben Everett was just one of the many thousands of lads who volunteered at sixteen or even earlier and went through the horrors of those years that tore the nation apart a century ago.

I am deeply indebted to a good friend, John J. Pullen, whose book, *The Twentieth Maine,* is not only an accurate historical account of a great regiment but a wonderfully readable story, as well. This book, together with the works of Bruce Catton, McKinlay Kantor, and other authorities on the Civil War, has given me invaluable background material for *The Muddy Road to Glory.*

I sincerely hope that young people who read my story will be moved to explore other books about this fascinating period in America's history and perhaps to visit some of the scores of battlefields where brave men from the North and South gave their lives for what they believed.

S. W. M.
1963

Contents

1	The Kennebec	11
2	The Rappahannock	22
3	Northward March	32
4	Gettysburg	40
5	Southward Again	51
6	Army Christmas	60
7	The Wilderness	69
8	Spotsylvania	81
9	The Chickahominy	90
10	Belle Isle	100
11	Escape	110
12	The James	120
13	The Petersburg	129
14	The Crater	138
15	Virginia Autumn	146
16	Another Spring	156
17	Appomattox	165
18	The Surrender	175
19	Home Again	184

The Muddy Road to Glory

1

The Kennebec

Ben Everett had turned sixteen just three days before it happened. He was cutting birches for firewood on a hillside that faced east toward Harmony Pond. It was a late February day in 1863—not too cold as Maine winter days went, but still frosty enough for clouds of steam to rise from his nose and mouth as he swung the ax. That morning he was working in what they called the South Woodlot, two miles below the family farm.

At ten-thirty or thereabouts, Ben began to get hungry. He had breakfasted before daylight and hiked down the road, carrying his ax, his pail of cold lunch, and a pair of snowshoes slung on his back. Now he had chopped and stacked up the better part of a cord of wood, and he felt he had earned a rest and a bite to eat. He went down to the big tree beside the road, where he had left his lunch and snowshoes, brushed the snow off a root, and sat down.

Ben was tall and gawky for his age. More than six feet in his socks, he weighed only a pound or two over a hundred and fifty. But working on the farm and cruising the woods had given him a wiry kind of strength. He had a tremendous appetite, too, and his mother often said he ate as much as two grown men.

Opening the lid of the five-pound lard pail, he looked inside appreciatively. On top was a wedge of apple pie, which he would save for dessert, but under it he found sandwiches —thick slabs of home-baked bread with slices of meat between. It was deer meat, from a buck he himself had shot. He was just taking the first big bite when he heard the jingle of sleigh bells from somewhere south along the road.

The bells didn't ring fast, the way they would have if the horse had been trotting. Whoever was coming was moving at a slow walk. He waited, sandwich in hand, to see who it might be, and as soon as the rig appeared, he recognized it. The plodding horse was familiar and so was the vehicle it pulled—a canvas-topped van, mounted now on sled runners. Across its side was painted the name of the itinerant peddler. "Zebulon Ricker," it said. "Pots, Pans and Sundries."

"Hi, Zeb!" Ben shouted, and the driver pulled up his horse.

"Wal," the little man called back, "if it ain't young Ben Everett! How's your folks?"

"All fine. You'll be seein' 'em 'fore I do, 'long as you're headed their way."

"How come you ain't in school, Ben?"

"Aw, I had a ruckus with the teacher. He was lickin' a little boy with a stick, an' I wouldn't let him. Then he set out to thrash me. I just left him lyin' on the floor an' come on home."

Ricker chuckled. "I bet your brother Abner didn't approve. Sent you down here to work an' cool off, eh?"

"Somethin' like that," Ben agreed. "What's the news from the war?"

"Not much. Army o' the Potomac's in winter quarters somewheres near the Rappahannock. Say—you remember Lawson Gray? He's a sergeant now. Seen him yesterday, down to Skowhegan."

"Wounded?" Ben asked.

"Naw—he's up here on furlough, recruitin' for the Twentieth Maine regiment. Ain't gettin' many, though. Bounties is too high in other towns. I guess he'll be goin' back tomorrow. Wal, Ben, looks like I got to be movin' on. See you soon."

Ben waved and went back to eating his sandwich, but instead of thinking how good it tasted, his mind was on something else. Ever since Lincoln's first call for volunteers, back in 1861, Ben had been crazy to join the Army. Then his father had died, and Abner became the head of the family. Ab was twenty-one, and he took a strict view of his responsibilities, especially in regard to disciplining his younger brother. Sternly he had forbidden Ben even to talk about enlisting. Abner himself had wanted to volunteer at first, but it was obvious that his duty was at home. And as long as Ben was under the draft age, he meant to keep him out of the fighting and on the farm where he belonged.

Now a growing excitement gripped the boy. Would there ever be another chance like this? He suddenly laid down the sandwich and started running up the road after the slow-moving peddler's van.

"Zeb," he panted when he drew abreast, "if you see my folks, tell 'em I won't be home. Here—take Abner this ax. I won't be needin' it, where I'm headed."

"Hmm," said Ricker, eyes wide with speculation. "I s'pose you know what you're a-doin'."

"Yep," Ben replied. And before the peddler could ask him any more questions, he was hurrying back to the woodlot. Perhaps what he planned to do was wrong. Abner would be furious, he knew, but he hoped his mother would understand. Sometimes she had sympathized with his burning desire to save the Union. If Zeb explained that the recruiting

officer was only there for a day, she might stand up for him, much as it would grieve her to have him risking his life.

He slung his snowshoes over his shoulder, picked up the still heavy lunch pail, and set off down the road. It was close to twenty miles from the place he had been working to the town of Skowhegan. More than that by the roads, but he knew some short cuts. By noon he had covered four miles,

swinging along at a steady woodsman's pace. Soon he came to a small river, known as the East Branch. The frozen surface was covered with snow, and he decided to use it for a highway, moving southward on his rawhide-webbed snowshoes. He stopped only once in the course of the afternoon to eat another sandwich and his pie. By the time the early twilight fell, he was in sight of the church steeples in the town.

Skowhegan was a fairly important place, standing as it did at the big bend of the Kennebec. Rafts of pine logs came down the river to be sawed into lumber at the mills, and the loggers spent their money there when they came out of the woods. Ben knew his way around the town. It took only a few minutes to locate the hotel where Sergeant Gray was staying, and he found the soldier in the lobby, about to go into the dining room to supper.

"Mr. Gray—Sergeant—you remember me?" said Ben diffidently. "I'm one o' the Everett boys from up Harmony way."

Lawson Gray was in his thirties, a keen-eyed, leathery-faced man in a uniform that was worn and faded but clean. He looked the youngster over and grinned.

"Sure," he said. "You're the youngest one—Ben, your name is. I used to go fishin' with your pa, but you weren't more'n knee-high to a grasshopper, those days. You've shot up some. How 'bout a bite o' vittles? I was just on my way to eat."

Awkwardly Ben followed him into the hotel dining room, and they sat down at the long table. The food was good, home-cooked and plentiful, and after his long hike Ben was hungry.

"Like to see a boy eat," said the sergeant appreciatively. "Down in Virginia, where I been, the grub's sort o' plain. But the young fellers like you seem to make out pretty good on hardtack an' beans."

"Th-that's what I wanted to see you about," said Ben, flushing. "I know I'm big enough an' strong enough, an' I want to go soldierin'."

"How old are you?" Gray asked him sternly.

Ben gulped. "Old enough," he mumbled.

"Wal, I don't like a boy to have to lie, so I won't press the matter. We'll say you're eighteen. I heard your father'd died. What do your ma an' your brother think o' your enlistin'?"

"I guess Ma'd say it's all right. Abner prob'ly wouldn't like it. I left word I was leavin' home when I heard you were here."

Gray took only a moment to make up his mind. "All right," he said. "I reckon we can make a soldier out o' you. But I want you to know what you're gittin' into. It's not just the fightin' that's tough. There's long marches when you're so tired you're ready to drop in your tracks. There's poor rations an' sometimes none at all. There's rain an' mud an' misery. An' on top of all that, there's the Rebs, snipin' at your head from behind their breastworks or makin' a surprise attack, yellin' their lungs out. But what good's it do to tell a boy all that? You got a place to sleep? If not, come bunk in with me. We'll be startin' south first thing tomorrow."

Very little that the sergeant had said made any impression on Ben. The main thing was that he was going to be allowed to enlist! He lay on a cot in Gray's room that night, too excited to go to sleep. At last weariness overcame him, and he slumbered soundly till dawn.

"Come on, there!" He heard the soldier's gruff voice. "It's near sunup—time to roll out. Soon as we've had breakfast, I'll take you down to the recruitin' office."

Ben scrambled out of the covers, scrubbed his face and hands at the washstand, and pulled on his clothes in a hurry.

"I'm sorry, Mr. Gray," he said. "I've got no money with me for my board an' lodging. Maybe you could trust me till I get my first pay."

"No need," the sergeant replied. "I can charge it off to recruitin' expenses."

By seven o'clock they were on their way to the post office for the swearing-in ceremony. There was a very brief medical examination by a bored-looking doctor in rumpled clothes. If a man looked healthy, he was usually taken without question. Only two other recruits showed up that morning, but Gray seemed satisfied. One of the pair was a lad of nineteen whom Ben knew—a fair-complexioned farm youngster named Loring Hawkes. He greeted Ben with a shy grin.

"Golly," he said, "it's good to have a friend comin' along! I didn't realize you was old enough to jine."

"Sh!" Ben told him warningly. "Far's you're concerned, Loring, I'm your age, or close to it."

They stood together while the third recruit was being entered on the rolls. He was a fat, unpleasant-looking youth of twenty, with a pimply face and shifty eyes. His name, they soon learned, was Perley Snell, and he gave his home town as Portland.

"Bet he's a bounty-jumper," Hawkes whispered. "Else why'd he come way up here to enlist?"

A bounty-jumper, Ben knew, was a man who enlisted and took the bounty money in one place, then deserted and went somewhere else to repeat the process.

Sergeant Gray marched them up the street to the town hall, and there each recruit was given his bounty of $100 in greenbacks. The thought of being rewarded for serving his country had never entered Ben's mind. He stared at the wad of bills in amazement.

"Ha!" Snell laughed. "Better put that stuff in yer pocket 'fore somebody steals it!"

Gray stepped over to Ben's side. "He's right," he told the boy. "But if I was you, I'd send some of it home to your folks. Make 'em feel a bit better about what you've done."

Ben was grateful for the advice. He kept only $20 for himself and mailed the rest to his mother. By that time it was nearly nine o'clock, and the train stood puffing in front of the station. The sergeant ushered them aboard, keeping an especially watchful eye on the recruit from Portland.

"All aboard!" called the conductor, and a moment later the wheels began to turn. Ben sat by the window, absorbed in the view of the Kennebec Valley. It was not only his first ride in the "cars" but also his first trip south of Skowhegan. They reached Augusta about noon, ate lunch there in the dirty little depot restaurant, and four or five hours later the train pulled into Portland. This was the biggest city Ben and Loring had ever seen, and they hurried out to stand on the platform, marveling at the brick stores and office buildings and the constantly moving stream of drays and carriages.

"Where's that other feller—that Snell?" Ben asked, looking around.

"The sergeant wouldn't let him git out with us." Hawkes chuckled. "I guess he don't trust him no more'n I do. Now he's got his bounty money, he's likely to skedaddle, first chance he sees."

Shortly Gray and Snell joined them. "Get your things out o' the car," said the sergeant. "We have to stop off here long enough to draw your blankets an' uniforms. They're issued by the State o' Maine."

At the local armory each of them drew a rough gray Army blanket and was fitted, after a fashion, with the light blue trousers and dark blue jackets worn by Union soldiers. To get the legs and sleeves long enough, Ben had to take a uniform several sizes too big around. But he figured by belting the loose pants tightly and setting the blouse buttons over, he would look passably like a fighting man. The caps they received were blue, with square black visors and a curled brass hunting horn on the front.

"You're goin' to be in my regiment, the Twentieth

Maine," said Gray. "That's part o' the Third Brigade, First Division o' the Fifth Corps. All First Division men git a red Maltese cross to sew on the top o' their caps. You'll be given that when you draw your muskets, in Washin'ton."

They stayed in Portland another hour—long enough for the young recruits to make a few purchases. Ben bought himself a small "housewife"—a cloth sewing case with needles, thread, and a pair of cheap scissors. Then the sergeant herded the little group down to the wharf and aboard the steamboat for New York.

It took two nights and a day to reach the sprawling metropolis on the island of Manhattan. Loring Hawkes was seasick most of the voyage, but Ben, who had never seen the ocean before, felt fine after the first hour or two. The four of them all bunked together in a low-priced cabin down next to the engines, and the heat and the clank of the huge walking beam overhead allowed them little sleep.

Daytime was better, for Ben stood up in the bows and watched the dunes of Cape Cod across the cold, heaving seas. Finally, at noon of the second day, the steamer came puffing up the East River and was warped into her berth.

"Stick close to me now," Gray ordered. "Easy to git lost 'tween here an' the railroad ferry, an' the whole place is swarmin' with roughs an' pickpockets. Sodom an' Gomorrah was peaceful towns 'longside o' New York."

Snell hung back, glancing around as if he wanted to bolt, but the sergeant had his arm in a firm grip.

"You've enlisted, young feller," he growled, "an' I aim to see you in the Army."

*   *   *

They rode all that night and part of the next day on the smoky wooden cars of the Pennsylvania Railroad. There were delays in Philadelphia and again in Baltimore. Ben was thoroughly sick of trains when at last they clattered into Washington. It wasn't as imposing a city as he expected, but it had a busy, military air that thrilled him. Soldiers were everywhere. He saw puffed-up colonels and majors strutting around the streets in well-pressed uniforms with sparkling gold buttons. Privates, non-coms, and officers of company rank seemed to be fewer in number—probably, he guessed, because they were at the front.

On their way to the U.S. Arsenal they had at least a glimpse of the Capitol, with scaffolding around its half-finished dome. There were no bands playing to greet the new recruits. Dirty snow lay in the gutters, and the streets were slimy with mud.

Gray checked his charges in at the arsenal, and a fat, bored-looking corporal handed each of them a new rifle and a leather cartridge box. Then, without even stopping to eat, Gray took them down to board a military steamer that lay tied up at a dock in the Potomac.

Fifty or sixty other recruits—draftees and volunteers—shouted sour jokes at the newcomers from the rail. Some of them didn't look very prepossessing. There were a few drunks and several big, strapping plug-uglies in the lot. A nervous young lieutenant ordered them to stand back and give the sergeant's squad room to come up the gangway.

Most of the group obeyed grudgingly, and as soon as the Maine men were aboard, a blast of the whistle announced the boat's departure. Then, as the paddle wheels roiled the brown water and the gap widened between the side and the dock, a burly, bearded man made a sudden dive over the rail. It all happened so quickly that Ben hardly had time to draw a breath before a shot rang out. The man in the river yelled once and turned over, floating face down. And the guard who had killed him calmly reloaded his rifle.

2

The Rappahannock

Ben and Loring were both too shaken to speak. They stood on the deck, staring back at the bubbles that rose where the man had sunk.

"Come on, boys," said Gray in a dry voice. "The feller had it comin'. That's what happens to deserters, an' I reckon he wasn't fit to be a soldier anyways. You, Snell, jest remember what you've seen."

They heard later that the dead man was a New York criminal who had enlisted to escape arrest and had given trouble all the way down on the train. According to the harsh Army regulations of the time, the guard had no choice but to shoot him when he tried to get away.

Steaming rapidly down the Potomac, the crowded steamboat reached Aquia Creek by sunset and nosed her way in to one of the long docks that lined the bank. There were huge piles of military goods there, and a lot of noise and activity, for this was the main supply route for Fighting Joe Hooker's Army of the Potomac.

The recruits were fed in a big mess tent and then rolled up in their blankets on the board floor of a temporary barracks building. Gray laughed when he saw the farm boys trying to make themselves comfortable on the hard planks.

"This is the best bed you're likely to have for a spell," he told them. "Wait till you try sleepin' in snow an' mud at the end of a long day's march!"

They were roused by bugle calls early next morning and fell into columns along with two or three hundred other recruits. After roll call they were given a breakfast of bread, fried pork, and coffee and lined up again, each man loaded down with his knapsack, haversack, blanket roll, and rifle. It was a cold, cloudy March morning, and a few drops of rain began to fall.

"Reg'lar Virginia marchin' weather," Sergeant Gray commented. "An' you'll git your first taste o' marchin' right now. Not too fur—it ain't but a dozen miles or so to Stoneman's Switch, an' that's where the Twentieth Maine's quartered."

An hour later the whole contingent of recruits had formed into three companies and were slogging southwestward through the mud. Their packs seemed to grow heavier and heavier with each mile they marched. Stragglers began to fall behind but were rounded up and pushed on by the harsh-voiced veteran sergeants and corporals. Several times they had to get off the road to let trains of food and ammunition wagons pass, and the green columns got a few minutes of welcome rest.

At last, about midafternoon, they came in sight of the vast encampment at Stoneman's Switch. It stretched for miles—street after street of tents and huts as far as the eye could see. The whole Army of the Potomac was in winter quarters here, and thanks to General Hooker's energetic management, the place was neat, orderly, and well-policed.

Ben had little time to marvel at what he saw. The recruits were promptly marshaled into some kind of ranks, and as the roll was called, each man was assigned to a military unit. Soon the two farm boys found themselves standing awkwardly in

the little tent that served as headquarters for Company B, Twentieth Maine Volunteers.

"At ease!" ordered the brisk young captain behind the folding table. "I'm Captain Morrill, your company commander, and I'm a Maine man, too. You can be proud of your regiment. Some day you'll hear how the Twentieth Maine acquitted itself at Fredericksburg. Right now, though, your job is to learn to be soldiers. Sergeant Gray will see to that."

He set down their names on the rolls and sent them off to find their quarters on the company street. Ben and Loring were assigned to a hut with two other privates, both veterans of more than a year's service. Their names were Ike Bean and Martin Preble. Ike was a short, thick-set man with tremendous arms, who had been a blacksmith in a lumber camp up on the Penobscot. Martin came from Boothbay Harbor, where he had helped his father at the fishing and lobstering. He was barely nineteen, but hardship and battles had worn him down, made him look older.

"You fellers are lucky," Ike told the newcomers. "We got a nice, trim place here an' expect you to help keep it that way. You won't have to live on hardtack, neither—not till the spring campaignin' starts. One thing we get here is soft bread, fresh baked. So make the most of it, whilst you can."

The ground inside the log hut was covered with clean straw to a depth of several inches, making a fairly comfortable place to sleep. No rain came through the stout canvas of the roof, and a ditch around the hut kept the floor dry.

It was Preble who showed them where to stow their gear and undertook to teach them how a rifle should be treated. Ben had done a lot of hunting and thought of himself as a good shot, but he soon discovered that in the Army there was more to it than that.

"When you're in the line an' facin' a mess o' Rebs," the

young fisherman explained, "you have to load an' fire pretty fast. What you got to do is practice loadin' in nine counts— like this. One, reach in your ca'tridge box an' pull out a fresh ca'tridge. Two, bite off the paper on the end. Three, pour the powder in the barrel. Four, put in the ball, with the pointed end on top. Five, pull the ramrod out o' the pipes. Six, ram the ball clear down. Seven, stick the ramrod back in its pipes. Eight, pull the hammer back to half-cock an' take off the old cap. Nine, git a new one out o' the cap pouch an' push it down on the nipple. Time you've got so you can do that in your sleep, you'll be ready for a battle.

"There's one more thing," he added. "Don't forgit it's loaded. I've seen green men forgit to fire their musket in a hot fight, an' first thing you know they'd loaded her clean to the muzzle with dear knows how many charges."

The rain had stopped before reveille the next morning, and the first thing they did was line up in front of the huts for inspection. Then they lined up again at the cookhouse to get their tin plates filled for breakfast. And a few minutes after eating they were marched out to the drill field, where Sergeant Gray took the new men aside to teach them the rudiments.

They were a clumsy bunch to start with. Some didn't know their right foot from their left, and they walked and stood with a natural farmer's slouch. Gray was firm but patient. Inside an hour he had most of the recruits straightening their backs and squaring their shoulders when they stood at attention. After that he started with the simplest elements of close-order drill.

Two days later the squad was considered fit to drill with the rest of the regiment. Ben and his friend Hawkes were put in the same platoon of B Company, but they were surrounded by more experienced soldiers. This proved to be a sound idea, for the veterans knew all the maneuvers by heart, and though Ben was occasionally cursed for his awkwardness, he felt that he was learning fast.

There was no effort to teach marksmanship. Most men in those days were familiar with how to aim a gun, and ammunition was too scarce to waste. However, hours were spent on the manual of arms and in going through the motions of loading and firing.

During the winter there had been a good deal of sickness in camp. Now, with warmer spring weather, most of the men in the regiment were reporting for duty, and the ranks, when drawn up on parade, contained nearly five hundred soldiers. This was far from the original regimental quota but a respectable number as war-worn regiments went in those days.

On the fourth Sunday after he reached camp, Ben wrote a letter to his mother, back in Maine. He told her he hoped she had received his bounty money safely and that Abner felt better, by now, about his enlisting.

"Things are pretty good here," he wrote. "I'm getting enough to eat and keeping in good health. The cooking is a long way short of yours, but that is to be expected in the Army.

"I figure you would be right proud to see me in uniform and doing drill. Last week the whole Army paraded for President Lincoln, and it was quite a sight. He looked sort of sorrowful and peaked, I thought, and he was on a small horse, so his long legs hung down most to the ground. Just the same, we all did our best to stand straight, and we gave him a cheer when he went by with Gen. Hooker.

"I keep my socks and underclothes as clean as I can, and you can be sure I say my prayers every night. I wish I had had a proper chance to tell you good-by. So far I have not been homesick, but I think of you pretty often. Your loving son, Benjamin.''

If he had written a week later, he might have had more news. Like all the rest of the Army, the Twentieth Maine had to be vaccinated for smallpox, and Ben's arm was scratched and he was inoculated along with the rest. Then something began to go wrong. By the seventeenth of April so many of the Maine men were down with real cases of the dread disease that the surgeon was afraid of a general epidemic. After three or four of the patients had died, it was decided that the regiment must be kept in quarantine, away from the rest of the brigade.

Ben was among the lucky ones. His scab itched for a few days, but he had no further trouble. Loring Hawkes, on the other hand, developed a high fever and was in the camp hospital for more than a week before he recovered. The trouble, everybody said, was a shipment of bad vaccine.

Meanwhile, the Army of the Potomac was preparing for a big attack on Lee's forces. Column after column, they marched away up the Rappahannock, every man with three days' rations and extra rounds of ammunition. Everybody was in high spirits, for this was to be the battle that would win the war.

It was pretty discouraging for the Twentieth Maine to be the only regiment left behind. Instead of going off to fight, they were assigned to guard the telegraph line between Falmouth and United States Ford. For a long, hot week they patrolled the vital dozen miles of wire, hearing good news from the front that made them wish more than ever they could have a share in the fighting. Then, early in May, the news was good no longer. Successful at first in their flanking attack at Chancellorsville, the Federals had suddenly been flanked themselves. Stonewall Jackson's tough army had handed them a crushing defeat. Soon Ben and his comrades saw crowds of badly disorganized Union troops stumbling past to the rear.

Right after Chancellorsville the morale of the Army of the Potomac dropped as low as it had been high a month before. Ben felt miserable and ashamed, almost as if he had been personally to blame. Colonel Ames, the West Pointer who had commanded the regiment ever since it was formed, was made a brigadier about that time, and his second in command, Joshua Chamberlain, was promoted to full colonel and took over the dispirited Twentieth Maine.

Some of the newer men doubted Chamberlain's ability. After all, he had been a college professor, and what did he know about fighting? But the veterans who had seen him in action at Fredericksburg knew better. Soon he was to prove his qualities of leadership in ways that would convince them all.

One of the first things that happened to challenge the new colonel was in the area of handling men. The Second Maine, earliest regiment from the Pine Tree State, was being disbanded. Some of its soldiers had enlisted for only two years and were going home. Others, because of Army red tape, had had to sign up for three years, and it naturally seemed unfair to them that their friends were getting discharges. A large contingent—a hundred and twenty men—of this three-year group was transferred to the Twentieth Maine in late May. Most of them were angry and mutinous.

Chamberlain was under orders to shoot any of them who refused to obey commands. Instead, he got permission to deal with the trouble in his own way. He found that the men from the Second Maine had been given nothing to eat for three days, and the first thing he did was order a good meal for them. After that their names were put on the company rolls, breaking them up into small groups throughout the regiment. Then he talked to them.

Their claims to discharge would be fairly investigated, he promised. Meanwhile, they would be treated not as mutinous prisoners but as soldiers in a well-run regiment. After all, he was a Maine man himself, and he understood the spirit of Maine men—not liking to be pushed around.

All but a half dozen of them agreed to cooperate and soon became staunch members of the outfit, while the handful who refused were held for court-martial. By his good sense in handling a touchy situation, Colonel Chamberlain had added real strength to his regiment and won new respect from his men.

As June came in along the Rappahannock, Ben marveled at the midsummer heat, so different from a Maine spring. On moonlight nights he heard the mockingbirds singing like mad in the trees—a new experience for a northern boy. Virginia, he thought then, was a pretty nice place to be.

The Twentieth Maine was now on picket duty at United States Ford, and right across the river, a long stone's throw away, they could see the Confederate pickets. On hot days the men of both armies went swimming. Often two naked youngsters, one from the North, the other from the South, would get together in midstream and talk and joke about the war. There was a kind of unwritten agreement that enlisted men wouldn't shoot at each other while picketing.

Ben had always been a good swimmer, and he thoroughly enjoyed this kind of soldiering. Several times he encountered a young Rebel named John Ellington, a North Carolinian whose southern drawl was amusing to New England ears. Coffee was one of the things the South had little of, and one day Ben carried a small waterproof bag of it out to his Tarheel friend. Ellington, in turn, gave him a plug of Carolina tobacco, which Ben traded to Sergeant Gray for some candy. One of Ben's accomplishments was his ability to imitate voices and accents. When he talked like Ellington, his tent-mates were convulsed.

"You better be careful," Ike Bean told him. "Somebody'll hear you talkin' like that an' shoot you fer a Reb."

Military secrets were not guarded very carefully in conversations between pickets. Ben told Ellington the name of his regiment and division and was impressed when he learned that the other lad had marched with Jackson's famous "foot cavalry."

"But ol' Stonewall's daid now," the youngster said bitterly. "None o' you Yanks could do it. 'Twas a wild Confederate shot as hit him, after we'd made y'all run at Chancellorsville."

"Too bad," Ben replied sincerely. "I guess he was quite a general. Well, Reb, take care o' yourself. If we ever come face to face in a battle, I hope none o' my bullets hits you."

Ellington laughed. "Same to you, Yank. I'll come see you in Maine after we win the war!"

3

Northward March

Though he had no way of knowing it, Ben's first pleasant months as a soldier were about over. He had been luckier than he realized. Now he had to learn the harsh realities of war.

After a few days the regiment's picket lines were shifted upriver to Ellis Ford, beyond the mouth of the Rapidan. Even to the enlisted men, it was soon apparent that fewer and fewer Confederates were to be seen on the opposite bank.

"Must ha' gone somewhere else," Martin Preble growled. "Old Lee's up to somethin', an' I bet we'll be marchin' any day now."

He was quickly proved right. On the sultry evening of June 13, the Twentieth Maine formed in columns of fours and after a short time caught up with the rest of the division at Morrisville. The next day dawned in stifling heat, but they set off early, marching under full pack. At Catlett's Station they joined the column of the Fifth Corps and moved on in a great river of dusty, blue-clad men.

By that time some of the recruits were having trouble keeping up the hard pace. Red-faced and gasping, Loring Hawkes unslung his pack and fell down to rest under a tree. "I'll try —an' ketch up," he panted to his comrades. And sure enough, late that night he staggered into their bivouac. His pack was lighter, for he had thrown away his blanket, haversack, and an iron frying pan that had been one of his treasures.

Ben had managed to keep up. He found his Army boots chafed his heels after a few miles, and he took them off, knotting the laces and hanging them around his neck with the socks stuffed inside. For years he had gone barefoot all summer, and his soles were still tough. While some of the other men got big raw blisters, he walked in comparative comfort. The swinging stride of the Army route-step came naturally to him, and the heat didn't bother his long, lean frame so much as it did the fatter recruits.

On the second day the cook-wagons fell hopelessly behind. All the men had to eat that night was hardtack and a little smoked beef. Many of the canteens were dry, too. Whenever the marchers passed a farmyard well, groups of men dropped out to get a hurried drink.

Hungry, thirsty, and tired, Ben fell into his blanket that night and was soon sleeping the sleep of exhaustion. The smell of coffee, hot and black, woke him at sunup. Some of the more provident members of the squad had coffee and a battered pot in their packs, and the brew proved to be just the thing to revive their spirits.

They passed the old battlefield of Bull Run that day, and Ben saw rusty guns, tattered bits of uniform, whitening bones, and smashed artillery wheels littering the ground. The untried men found little to cheer them in the gruesome scene.

It grew hotter and hotter. On the march from Manassas to Gum Spring, four soldiers died from sunstroke and nearly half the regiment dropped out of ranks to come hobbling in many hours later. The Twentieth Maine didn't know just where it was going, but somebody higher up—maybe General Hooker—must be in an almighty big hurry.

On the eighteenth of June, the tired bluecoats got a chance to rest, fill their canteens, and even eat a little real food. So far their march had been on a line almost due north. Now, after the short respite, they fell into ranks once more and turned to the west. Off there on the horizon was a range of hills that Ben heard the veterans call the Bull Run Mountains. Lee's Army of Northern Virginia, it seemed, was somewhere on the other side of those hills, hurrying northward. And a sound of distant firing told the Maine soldiers that there was some kind of a skirmish up ahead.

Ben had seen very little of Perley Snell since the trip down from Portland, for he had been put in another company. That day, however, he caught a glimpse of the mean-faced youth beside the road. Snell was being dragged along by a couple of provost guards and apparently had thrown away his rifle and knapsack.

"What you got there?" Sergeant Gray called to the guards.

"Just another skulker," one of them replied with a grin. "Found him hidin' in the woods. Must ha' heard the shootin' an' decided he wanted to go home."

The rest of the regiment was doing better than on previous days. The country was higher and a little cooler now. While the ranks had been thinned by sore feet and illness, those who were left pushed on eagerly toward whatever fighting was in progress.

That evening, as they approached the little town of Aldie, at the foot of a gap in the hills, they heard that Jeb Stuart and his hard-riding Rebel cavalry had been there. A Union force had driven them back through the gap, but they were still too close—only a few miles away, near Middleburg.

The Twentieth Maine bivouacked at Aldie. In the morning

they saw a column of Federal cavalry trot past, going over
to probe Stuart's position. There was distant firing, but it
wasn't until the next day that infantry support was sent for.
The job fell to Vincent's Brigade, of which the Maine men
were a part. At three in the morning Ben and his mates
were ordered out. His hands trembled a little as he strapped
on his knapsack and made sure he had a full cartridge case.
At last he was going into battle.

By the time daylight came, the brigade had passed Middleburg and could see dismounted gray horsemen waiting for
them in the fields west of the town. They would have to attack uphill. And facing them were the muzzles of six Confederate cannon. As they formed into line of battle, one of their
four regiments—the Eighty-third Pennsylvania—disap-
peared mysteriously into the woods at the left. Then the
bugle sounded, and the three remaining regiments started
their advance.

Ben felt a cold sweat running down his neck, but he pushed
forward with the rest. The artillery was blasting, and shells
screamed close overhead, while from behind the stone walls
there came the flashing, snapping fire of the Rebels' cavalry
carbines. The second man to the right in the line stumbled,
spun around once, choked, and lay still. Ben's immediate in-
stinct was to turn and run. What was he doing here? Why—a
fellow could get hurt—even killed! But he kept going, guid-
ing on the colors.

There was something steadying about the sight of those
faded, bullet-riddled flags, so firmly held.

At last, when they had covered more than half the distance,
the welcome order came to start firing. A yell went up from
the Yankee line and answering bullets began flying toward
the enemy. Ben drew a shaky bead on a gray-uniformed captain standing behind the wall and squeezed the trigger. He

saw the officer drop his saber and grab the arm that had been waving it. Then, even as he reloaded, another yell sounded on the Confederate flank, and the Pennsylvania regiment came boiling out of the woods. Caught by surprise, the Rebels turned and started to retreat.

Just at that moment Ben heard a jarring thunder of hoofs behind him, and the line parted hastily to let the Union cavalry go through. It was a magnificent sight—horses at a gallop, sabers swinging, bugles sounding the charge. The blue horsemen swept through the departing Rebel troops like a scythe through grain, and soon that particular fight was over, as far as the foot soldiers were concerned.

Forty or fifty Confederate prisoners were rounded up, as well as one of the guns that had been abandoned. But there was little time to gloat over the victory. Almost at once the brigade formed up again to march in the wake of the cavalry.

"How'd you make out, Ben?" Martin Preble asked. "Git you a Johnny Reb?"

"I hit one—an officer he was, too. But I guess I just winged him. Hope so, anyhow. Killin' folks don't seem to be as much fun as it's cracked up to be."

After a couple of miles the brigade had to go into line of battle once more. Stuart's cavalry, it seemed, was merely teasing them—luring them farther and farther across the valley. Again they charged, and again the Rebels retreated. Finally, in midafternoon, the four Union regiments had pushed the enemy back six miles. Tired as they were, they couldn't bivouac there, in the shadow of the Blue Ridge and Lee's main army. They had to turn and march back toward Aldie while the Yankee cavalry continued the chase as far as Ashby's Gap.

With them the foot soldiers carried their casualties, one

man killed and nine wounded. As Ben was to discover later, the Twentieth Maine always buried its own dead.

Back on the east side of the Bull Run Mountains, they had three days of rest. Ben had a chance to wash his grimy shirt and socks in a little stream and to think back over his first experience under fire. He had a good feeling about it. Never again, he thought, would he be tempted to run away from the fighting. Certainly he had no wish to be another Perley Snell—a real disgrace to a good regiment.

The hot weather broke on the twenty-sixth of June, and it began to rain dismally. As the brigade fell into line of march, Ben pulled his poncho over his head to keep his rifle and uniform dry, but his legs were soon dripping. They tramped twenty miles that day, sloshing through the mud. Before evening they crossed the Potomac at Edwards Ferry and made a wet camp at Poolesville, a few miles north of the river in Maryland.

The officers were growing jittery now. Something big was evidently afoot, and the infantry grapevine passed the word that Lee's whole force was ahead of them, marching into Pennsylvania and threatening to attack Philadelphia—Baltimore—even Washington itself.

The next day's march brought them to the outskirts of Frederick, where they got another day's respite. Some of the soldiers went into the town and bought food to bring back to camp. Along with it they brought news. It was true that Lee was now well into Pennsylvania, and the whole North was scared. Also, for some reason none of the enlisted men quite understood, Fighting Joe Hooker had been fired, and General Meade, commander of the Fifth Corps, was now in charge of the whole Army of the Potomac. By that time the veterans were used to such shifts in command. They had served under the popular "Little Mac" McClellan, then

Burnside, then Hooker. As far as they were concerned, Meade was as good as any of them. He had proved he was brave and had good sense. Nobody who had been in the ranks very long expected any miracles from Union leadership. Names of Confederate generals like Lee and Jackson and Longstreet carried more respect among the Yankee soldiers than those of their own top commanders.

Meade's decision, apparently, was to keep between Lee and the big Northern cities and get ready for a battle wherever the two forces might meet. That, as the Twentieth Maine quickly discovered, meant more hard marching.

For the next three days, up to and including the first of July, the regiment averaged more than twenty miles a day— and on the last day made twenty-six miles. By that time the ranks were stripped of all but the toughest and healthiest men. Ben got pretty tired on those marches, but he was proud that he could stand up to it.

Each evening it was a grateful bunch of soldiers who heard the order to "fall out for bivouac" come echoing back along the column. As soon as they had stacked their arms, several men from each squad scurried around gathering wood. Usually that meant fence rails, for they were in a country of farms rather than of forests. A lot of angry farmers had to rebuild miles of fences once the Army had passed.

Over the little campfires, coffee was soon boiling and salt pork sizzling in frying pans among the coals. The only bread they had was the much-hated hardtack, which was a test for teeth and digestion but did furnish some nourishment.

Few men had the energy to linger around the fires after supper. As long as the weather held fair, they didn't bother with shelter tents but flung themselves down on their ponchos and blankets and were quickly lost in slumber. Ben had slept out in the open many times as a boy in Maine. His limber body never felt the bumps in the ground, and he thought clean, fresh, grassy earth made a pretty good bed.

On that last long day of the northward march, the Twentieth Maine was out in front as advance guard. They moved with skirmishers out on both sides, and for miles behind them the Fifth Corps came tramping up the dusty road.

It was beautiful country—that farmland above the Maryland-Pennsylvania line. The farther north they went, the more friendly faces they saw. There was milk for sale along the roadside, and a few patriotic women gave them pies and doughnuts. Then, as they came close to the town of Hanover, they found signs of recent fighting. There were dead horses and dead cavalrymen lying in the road, for Jeb Stuart and his fast-riding Rebels had been there before them. More than ever they had an ominous feeling that a big battle must be coming soon.

That sense of uneasiness grew stronger late in the afternoon, when they bivouacked a little way beyond Hanover. The air shook, as if thunder was rolling too far away to hear. Hardly had the campfires been lighted when a courier on a lathered horse came galloping down the road, and in a few minutes the word had spread through all the ranks. Lee's Army of Northern Virginia was less than fifteen miles to the west and had already beaten the First Corps and the Eleventh Corps at a place called Gettysburg.

Without even time to eat, the weary soldiers were lined up again and set off northward. It was after midnight when they were told to halt and take a few hours of rest. As soon as the sun rose on the second of July, the bugles roused them once more, and they staggered into battle formation with all the other units of the Fifth Corps.

4

Gettysburg

Through the slanting light of early morning, they waded forward, crossing fields of wheat and oats and hay. After a while they mounted a rise of ground that gave them a view of low, wooded hills ahead. The sides of these hills were crisscrossed with earthworks, hastily thrown up during the night, and there were a multitude of wagons, guns, and limbers at the foot of the slope. The hills were where the main battle line must be.

Ben's regiment lined up in formation with the Fifth Corps. He couldn't see the little town where yesterday's fighting had taken place, for it was hidden by the hilltops to the north and west. Colonel Chamberlain, in command of the Twentieth, strode out in front of the ranks and read the orders that had come from Meade's headquarters. From the solemn words and the Colonel's grim face, they knew that this must be an important battle—perhaps the showdown fight that would see the Union saved or broken.

After an hour or two, the Fifth Corps was moved to a reserve position back of Powers Hill, near the Baltimore Pike. There were occasional reports of cannon and a faint sound of musketry like distant firecrackers. Just skirmishers, they decided, and lay down beside their rifles to rest. It was hot and they were tired.

Thanks more to luck than to planning, the Union Army held a good position that day. Driven back from the town of Gettysburg, they now occupied a fishhook-shaped range of hills, running from Culp's Hill on the north, down the length of Cemetery Ridge, to Little Round Top and Big Round Top at the southern end. Lee's forces were over on the other side of a shallow valley two miles wide, and they, too, were on a stretch of high ground known as Seminary Ridge. The names meant little to Ben at that moment, but he would remember them later.

If General Dan Sickles, commander of the Third Corps, hadn't disregarded Meade's orders, it is possible that the Maine men would not have seen action on that fateful day. Sickles had been told to hold the southern half of the ridge, including Little Round Top. Instead, he decided it was a poor position and pushed his corps forward through a wheat field and a peach orchard, almost to the Emmitsburg Road. This meant the whole left flank of the Union Army was left unprotected.

At first General Lee knew nothing about that fact, for he had no scouting force to tell him. Jeb Stuart's cavalry had gone off on a wild-goose chase toward Washington and wasn't available for reconnaissance. But Longstreet, on the Confederate right, saw through his field glasses that the Round Tops seemed to be the anchor of the line and suggested that his tough corps move around them to flank the Federals and take them in the rear. Lee, however, ordered him to move straight ahead. At last, on that morning of July 2, Longstreet was ready to start his march. He had to wait for one of his brigades to come up, and it was after three in the afternoon before his troops were in a position to attack.

Meanwhile, General Hood's Texas scouts had climbed to the top of Big Round Top and discovered there were no defenders at that end of the line! Also they saw hundreds of supply and ammunition wagons parked temptingly just east of the hills. So, at the very time the rest of Longstreet's corps was hitting Sickles' men in the peach orchard, Hood's division set off to the right, beyond the southern arm of Sickles' position. They would take the two vital hills and roll up the Union forces from the flank.

The Third Corps was in real trouble now, and word was sent back hurriedly to the Fifth Corps to come up and help. Ben Everett knew nothing of all this, of course. All he knew was the sudden order to get into line, and soon the Twentieth Maine was crossing the ridge, following Colonel Chamberlain toward the hot battle in the wheat field ahead. Then, to his surprise, the orders were changed. Somebody had to occupy Little Round Top before the Confederates reached it, and Vincent's Brigade was given the job.

Of the four regiments in the brigade, the Maine boys were the last to climb the rocky north face of the hill. Already the Rebels had brought their artillery fire to bear on the crest, and trees and limbs were flying in all directions as the shells burst. Quickly General Vincent moved his veteran regiments into position. The Twentieth Maine scrambled past the Sixteenth Michigan, the Forty-fourth New York, and the Eighty-third Pennsylvania and finally reached the southeast corner of Little Round Top. There they dug in grimly behind rocks and tree trunks and waited for the attack.

But Captain Morrill's B Company, of which Ben was a member, was no longer with them. At the Colonel's orders, they had gone on down the south slope of the hill in skirmish formation, with rifles at the ready. A moment later the fifty-odd men of Company B had started climbing again, this time up the slope of Big Round Top.

Panting in the heat, Ben and his companions had nearly

reached the summit when they saw other men in blue coming toward them through the trees, firing as they fell back. They were regular Army sharpshooters, and they were being driven off the hill by a much larger force of Confederates.

Morrill ordered Company B to join them in their orderly retreat. Just east of the narrow valley that lay between the two Round Tops, there was a stone wall that would give them cover. The Rebel fire died out as they left the foot of the bigger hill, and they were able to reach the wall in safety and crouch behind it.

By the time Ben had reloaded his rifle a terrific fight was developing on Little Round Top, where the rest of the Twentieth Maine was in position. General Law's brigade of five Alabama regiments plus the Fourth and Fifth Texas had overrun Sickles' men at the Devil's Den and now charged the hill. They were lean, tough soldiers in butternut and faded gray, and they stormed up the slope with battle flags flying, howling like a pack of wolves. Amazingly the thin blue line on the crest held them and flung them back. The slaughter on both sides was frightful to watch. Ben held his breath at the sight of men falling in hand-to-hand conflict or mowed down by rifle fire. Many of those who fell were friends of his —good friends, beside whom he had marched and fought. His finger itched on the trigger, but Captain Morrill had forbidden any firing.

"Steady, boys," he told them. "Keep out of sight and wait. You'll get your chance."

The Fifteenth Alabama was only a hundred yards away and hurrying to get behind the Maine regiment's flank. But Chamberlain had foreseen the move. Four companies had worked farther to the left, and by the time the Alabamians went panting up the hill toward what they thought was the undefended rear, they met with stout resistance.

It was a terrible thing to watch. Guns were fired almost muzzle to muzzle. Then, with no time to reload, blue soldiers fought gray with clubbed muskets—rocks—fists—whatever they could lay their hands on.

Numbers of the enemy reached the crest and even planted their flags there. But somehow they were always hurled back. For a long time the noise of the battle had been so loud that the men of Company B couldn't have talked to each other if they'd tried. They lay there behind the wall, staring up at the turmoil, sick with fear for their comrades. Then at last a quieter moment came as the Alabama troops stumbled down the hill to regroup for another attempt.

"By thunder!" Sergeant Gray muttered. "I b'lieve our boys are out o' ca'tridges!"

It was true. No more shots were coming from the Yankee line on the heights. Surely if they had ammunition, they would be using it now, while the Rebels were trying to catch their breath. But then a strange thing happened. Ben saw a few of the Maine men stand up, then others; then the regimental colors were lifted high. And suddenly, with a strangled yell, the ragged veterans of the Twentieth Maine were running down the hill! They were pitifully few—only about two hundred of them now—but they came like avenging angels, with gleaming bayonets fixed.

That charge was the last thing the Alabamians expected. In confusion they looked, huddled, pushed each other, tried to fall back. If any of their rifles were loaded, there was neither time nor room to fire. And at that moment Captain Morrill rose behind the stone wall.

"Now, men!" he yelled. "Let 'em have it!"

Ben stood up with the rest, leveling his Enfield and taking aim. It was impossible to get a sight on any one soldier in the milling gray mass, but the concentrated fire of Company B and the sharpshooters wrought terrible havoc among the Alabama and Texas troops. They had fought like tigers in their attempts to dislodge the Union brigade. In the struggle they had lost more than half their men and officers. Now, with bayonets in their faces and bullets in their backs, there was nothing they could do but run. In a moment the retreat turned into a rout, with every man for himself.

The ground they left was crimson with blood and almost solidly covered with dead and wounded. Moreover, the Twentieth Maine had taken nearly four hundred prisoners. For the moment, at least, Little Round Top was safely in Union hands, and the regiment of Maine men climbed back to its position, picking up its wounded and sending the prisoners to the rear.

It had been a great victory but a costly one. Of the three hundred and sixty men who had made up the regiment at the beginning of the battle, a hundred and thirty were dead or dying or in the crowded field hospitals. Colonel Strong Vincent, who had been in command of the brigade, was one of the casualties, and his place was taken by Colonel Rice, of the Forty-fourth New York.

Now it was growing dark, but the remnant of the Maine regiment still had work to do, for the heights of Big Round Top remained a threat to the Union left. If Rebel artillery should occupy it during the night, their guns could rake the whole length of Cemetery Ridge.

Through some error, no ammunition had been sent up, but the Twentieth Maine didn't wait for it. With bayonets still fixed, they started climbing the side of the bigger hill in the dark. As they neared the top, they found there were Confederates there before them.

Ben, with two other men from his squad, had been scrambling up the slope among rocks and brambles. At the

end of the climb, he almost stumbled over a Rebel picket, who was even more surprised than he was. Hastily Ben thrust the bayonet point within inches of the man's face.

"Keep still!" he whispered. "Drop your gun an' come with us!"

When the regiment formed a line of battle on the crest, Ben discovered that half a dozen other Confederates had been captured. Chamberlain passed the word quietly, and the Maine men moved forward in a solid front, their bayonets glittering in the starlight. To the eyes of the Rebel skirmishers, they must have looked like a whole division approaching, for without firing a shot the Southerners made a hasty departure down the west slope. Ben could hear the crackle of snapping twigs that marked their route.

The regiment's position was still dangerous, so Chamberlain detached Company B to act as a picket line and took the rest of the men back to a point nearer the foot of the hill. At the same time he sent a messenger for reinforcements and ammunition. Soon the Eighty-third Pennsylvania and the Forth-fourth New York came to join them, bringing enough cartridges to supply the Maine men with at least a few rounds.

It was only fair that Captain Morrill's company should have the picket duty that night. They had sat behind the wall while their comrades fought so desperately on Little Round Top. Now, with the weary regiment resting, they kept the watch.

Along with twenty others under Sergeant Gray, Ben crept down the southwest slope to reconnoiter. They were close enough to see the Rebels' fires and listen to their talk. As they started climbing back, they must have made enough noise to attract attention in the Confederate camp. Soon a squad from one of the Texas regiments came up to find out what was going on.

"Halt, now!" Ben challenged in his best imitation of a Southern voice. "Who goes thar?"

"Friends," the Texans replied.

"Advance an' be reco'nized."

A moment later the surprised Texans were silently disarmed and taken back to regimental headquarters. An hour later it happened again, and by a little after midnight twenty-five Rebel pickets had been captured.

After that more and more Union regiments came up to

join the Third Brigade, and the line was strong on both the hilltops before dawn. In the middle of the morning of July 3, the Maine regiment was withdrawn from Big Round Top and sent to a northward position, behind the center of the Federal line.

They had had only about three hours of sleep in the last two days and nights. Now, completely exhausted, they thought they might have a chance to rest while they lay in reserve. Yet it soon turned out that sleep was impossible. Never in his life had Ben heard such a deafening roar of artillery fire as began shortly after noon. Many of the Confederate shells came over the ridge and burst within yards of the Maine men.

Not until afterward did they know that the awful cannonade had been a prelude to Pickett's gallant charge. Fifteen thousand of the finest soldiers in Lee's army came across the fields to attack the Union center. Under terrible musketry fire, they marched in solid ranks right up to the smoking muzzles of the batteries on Cemetery Ridge. Behind strong earthworks, the blue-clad regiments waited for them, fought them hand to hand, and hurled them back. When the Confederates finally retreated, they left thousands of dead and mutilated men behind.

Though nobody seemed to realize it at the moment, that was the end of the battle of Gettysburg. Medics and stretcher-bearers from both sides went out to comb the fields that night and bring in the wounded. The hospital tents in the rear areas reeked with blood, and piles of amputated arms and legs rose higher than the operating tables.

On the morning of July 4, there were cautious probes by squads of Yankee skirmishers to discover what the Rebels were up to, but they found out nothing for certain.

It was early the next day when the Twentieth Maine and

the rest of the Third Brigade set out across the valley on reconnaissance. The weather was still fiercely hot, as it had been for a week, and thousands of dead men and horses lay where they had fallen, in the rocks of Devil's Den, in the wheat field and the peach orchard. Ben was so sickened by the sight and smell of those swollen corpses that he had to stop to vomit. And he wasn't the only one.

They went on, all the way to Seminary Ridge, and encountered not a single live enemy. When they returned, their officers were able to report that Lee had definitely pulled the Army of Northern Virginia out of the area.

"I calculate," Sergeant Gray remarked with a wry face, "that means we'll be marchin' again 'fore night."

5

Southward Again

There was a heavy thundershower that afternoon, turning to steady rain about the time the regiment was ordered into column of march. Most of the men were sure the downpour was caused by the cannonading of the past few days. Privately Ben figured it was the heat that brought it on. But in any case, the Army of the Potomac was soon slogging southward, wet to the skin.

The mud was slippery and a foot deep in many places. It clung to their boots, making a sucking sound at every step and weighting down their weary legs.

As darkness shut down, the men marched blindly in the rain and mist. The only way a soldier knew he was still in column was by listening to the squashy sounds of feet in the mud or bumping into the man in front.

It was midnight before the order to halt was given. The bone-tired members of Company B drove their bayonets into the ground and stretched shelter halves between two rifles. Fires were impossible in the rain, so they went to bed supperless, huddling in their blankets under the little tents. Mud, Ben thought, was soft enough to make a pretty good bed if you didn't mind being wet. He lay there and remembered meals he had eaten back at the farm in Harmony. It was a habit he had formed when his stomach yearned for something more than sodden, wormy hardtack.

First he remembered things his mother cooked around this time of year, in July. Stewed chicken and dumplings, new green peas, blueberry pie to eat with a big mug of milk. Or winter meals, after hog-killing time, when they would have rib-thick slices of tender roast pork, baked Maine potatoes, hot buttermilk biscuits, and two kinds of pie—mince and pumpkin—for dessert.

Sometimes, when the work was light and they could go fishing, there were great kettles of fish chowder, made with black bass or perch and gallons of buttery milk, flavored with crisped onions and bacon and potatoes. Then he remembered Saturday night suppers. How his mouth watered at the memory of beans, baked all day in a brick oven or a bean hole, enriched with succulent bits of fat pork and sweetened with molasses! With them there was always luscious steamed brown bread, spread with new-churned butter.

Luckily sleep overcame him in the midst of these feasts, and he dreamed blissfully of eating his fill of winter apples —red-cheeked Jonathans and sweet brown russets.

He woke at daybreak, with stiff muscles and hunger cramps in his stomach. The rain had let up enough for breakfast fires to be started, and Ben felt better after a cup of hot black coffee had washed down his hardtack.

They marched again that day, but not so far. Once more they went into bivouac in the late afternoon and looked hopefully back along the road for the supply wagons that hadn't yet caught up. There was still light enough for Ben to write another letter home.

"I guess I will be hearing from you soon," he told his mother. "We haven't got any mail from the North since I wrote you before, but there is quite a lot to tell. By this time you have probably heard about the Gettysburg battle. It was pretty bad, but you will be glad to know I came through safe. A lot of the other Maine boys got killed. There was Jim Esley and Fortune Doane of our company, and about sixty or seventy others in the regiment. Now we are trying to head off the Rebels before they can get back to Virginia. One thing I hate to tell you, because I know how you will take on, but all of us in the whole Army are lousy. Perhaps it ain't so strange, because marching all the time, we don't have any chance to wash or change our shirts. So we just keep scratching. If the sun ever comes out and we can get near a river or a brook, we'll take a bath and wash out some clothes. I am well and hope all at home are the same. Your loving son, Ben."

The statement about his health wasn't quite true, for in addition to lice and poor rations, Ben and most of his companions were suffering from diarrhea. Since he didn't know how to spell the word and had no wish to distress his mother further, he said nothing about it.

On the seventh of July, the Fifth Corps got moving again and marched a full twenty miles in the rain and mud, getting almost to Frederick before going into bivouac. Lee's army, so the enlisted men heard by the grapevine, was somewhere west around Antietam Creek, getting ready to cross the Potomac. That meant that to reach the enemy, the Union forces would have to cross two ridges of high hills—the Catoctins and the South Mountain range—and they knew a lot more marching was ahead.

Next day they swung westward. Just to vary the monotony of steady rain, they ran into a heavy thunderstorm that afternoon as they went panting up the rugged slopes of the Catoctin Mountains. Doggedly, they pushed on to the top, and suddenly a bright sun lighted up the valley ahead. Some of the older men in the regiment recalled coming this way before, on the way to their first big fight at Antietam the previous fall. It was prettier now, they said—all green fields and waving grain, where it had been dry, brown stubble before.

For days the Army of the Potomac moved forward, climbing South Mountain in hot sunshine and coming down toward Antietam Creek. They crossed that stream on the tenth. Lee's forces were still just ahead, dug in behind earthworks and unable to cross the Potomac because of high water from the recent rains. It began to look as if another big battle was shaping up—one that might decide the whole war.

After that they went on cautiously, with constant little fights between skirmishers thrown out by the two armies. Then, formed in a long line of battle, the Union troops moved in on Lee's position at Williamsport, and Ben thought it was quite a sight. There were thousands of blue-clad men marching to the beat of drums, regimental colors flying, every corps and division and regiment lined up in columns as if they were on parade.

Suddenly it began to rain again, and the advance came to a halt. The men bivouacked in the fields where they were, sure there would be a big fight on the morrow. But when morning dawned, the Confederates were gone. Somehow, in the night, the Army of Northern Virginia had managed to cross the swollen river.

*   *   *

The next three weeks turned out to be about as miserable a time as the Twentieth Maine had ever known. They were marched down the Maryland side of the Potomac to a place called Berlin, where the whole Army crossed into Virginia.

The Confederates were traveling down the west side of the Blue Ridge, and the Federals followed on the east. There were constant skirmishes between small detachments that tried scouting forays through the gaps.

It was July 23 when the Army of the Potomac nearly caught up with the enemy. Ben's division had marched hard and fast —so fast that the supply wagons were left far behind—and as they came in sight of Manassas Gap, the men were completely out of rations.

The Third Corps was sent ahead to drive the enemy's covering force out of the way, while the Fifth Corps, which included the Twentieth Maine, watched the attack from a knoll in the gap. After a brisk fight, the Third Corps found the Rebel line too tough to break and fell back, just before sunset.

Then the order came for the Fifth Corps to move up. The hungry Maine men fell into column and went on to the place where the other corps had started. There they were told to wait till morning before making a fresh attack.

That was a strange evening. No firing came from the Confederate lines, and the starving Yankees prowled the fields looking for vegetables or anything else that could be eaten. Ben managed to collect a mess of collard greens and four or five tiny new potatoes, which he shared with his tentmates. It wasn't very filling food, but it took the ravenous edge off their appetites, and afterward they were able to sleep.

At the break of day, they were routed out of their blankets and ordered forward, their stomachs grumbling with emptiness. The skirmish line took a lot of time to get anywhere, for every time they saw what looked like a vegetable, they stopped to pick it up. Finally, Ben's regiment began to move in line of battle. The slopes were steep—almost vertical in places—and covered with rocks, brush, and tangled blackberry vines. At the top they found masses of ripe blackberries, which they started picking with both hands. Martin Preble was only a yard or two from Ben as they gobbled the shiny black fruit.

"Sure taste good, don't they?" Preble mumbled with a full mouth. "Good for what ails your stummick, too. Eat enough o' these an' you won't have to go so much."

Whether this was true or not, there must have been some nourishment in the berries. Ben had enough energy to push on to the western edge of the hill and look out across the rich beauty of the Shenandoah Valley. It was as handsome country as he had ever seen, but it was completely empty of Rebel troops. The last divisions of Lee's army had passed southward in the night, and the covering force had pulled out to follow. That ended the action at the place the Union soldiers called "Molasses Gap." But Ben Everett would remember the feast of blackberries for a long time afterward.

Somebody had found a stray steer, lean and tough, and that night the men of Company B chewed on the stringy meat, broiled over their campfire. After that it started raining again, and though they had to sleep in the wet, the shower was over before morning.

The marching continued day after day as the Army of the Potomac went southward. It was hot, too. None of the Maine men had ever had to endure such humid, depressing heat as they found that summer in Virginia. After a week or two, the First Division of the Fifth Corps was back almost where it had started, on the banks of the Rappahannock. The Twentieth Maine went into camp there and was given the job of guarding Beverly Ford, just west of the Orange and Alexandria Railroad. It was a relief to have a chance to swim again and wash a few clothes. Besides that, they had enough to eat once more.

*   *   *

The Union Army was having its troubles with bounty-jumpers and deserters that summer. The draft law had given rise to a whole new crop of frauds. In the big cities like Boston, New York, and Philadelphia, there were many unscrupulous men who made a business of shanghaiing drunks and half-wits and handing them over to the draft boards, collecting the enlistment bounty for themselves. In other cases, thieves and pickpockets went into the Army a jump ahead of the law and then deserted at the first opportunity.

Any young man who had money and didn't want to fight could get out of being drafted by hiring a substitute for $300. Poorer people naturally resented this, and the feeling came to a head in gang-ruled New York, where a week of rioting resulted in the deaths of hundreds of men.

Because of all this, the quality of the replacements who joined the service was pretty miserable. And frequently half the draftees would disappear on the way from the North to Virginia.

Toward the end of August, something drastic had to be done. The Government in Washington agreed to have five recaptured deserters shot in front of the whole Fifth Corps, figuring that this was the best way to discourage others from trying it.

Ben recalled the occasion with horror all the rest of his life. The day was fair and the light breeze cool when the Twentieth Maine, with all the other regiments of the corps, marched out to form three sides of a huge hollow square. There was a slope to the ground, so that every man could see what happened, and nobody could turn his head away because they were standing at attention.

After a long, uneasy time, a muted band appeared, playing the death march. Behind the musicians came the Provost Marshal with a firing squad of fifty men. And finally they saw five coffins, each carried by four soldiers and followed by one of the chained prisoners. This grim parade moved slowly all around the square before it came to rest beside five open graves.

It took an almost intolerable time for the culprits to hear the prayers and exhortations of the clergymen, and the ranks of enlisted men stirred restlessly. After standing there for three hours, several soldiers fainted. At long last, when the hour neared four o'clock, the prisoners were blindfolded and placed in front of their coffins. And at the order, fifty rifle shots blasted the silence. The whole corps gave a shuddering gasp as the bodies crumpled.

Ike Bean cursed under his breath. "I've watched a heap o' men die on the battlefield." He choked. "But I never want to see nothin' like this again."

Nobody seemed to have much appetite for supper that night.

*　　*　　*

The August heat had put a good many soldiers in the hospital, and among those stricken with malaria was Colonel Joshua Chamberlain of the Twentieth Maine. He was replaced by Colonel Gilmore. When Chamberlain came back to active duty, he had been promoted to command of the Third Brigade—an honor his men felt was well deserved after what he had done at Gettysburg. They would miss him, but he was still their commander, and they knew he would always take a special interest in his old regiment.

Almost at once he started the brigade drilling, sprucing up uniforms and cleaning equipment. The other regiments, doubtful at first because he wasn't a West Pointer, soon came to respect his fairness and good discipline. And it wouldn't be long, Ben was sure, before they would learn to respect his fighting qualities as well.

Early in September the Army of the Potomac moved across

the Rappahannock and down the Orange Railroad to Culpeper Court House. There another month passed before the action of the fall campaign got under way.

Ben had escaped any major illness that summer, and since he had been getting enough to eat, his bony frame had filled out a little. There were no scales on which he could weigh himself, but he figured he must be five or six pounds heavier than when he left home. When the command came for the regiment to put itself in marching order, he was actually glad of the change.

6

Army Christmas

As long as the Union Army had stayed down near Fredericksburg, supplies could come by boat to Aquia Creek and be hauled in wagons to the front. But Culpeper Court House was thirty miles or more to the west. That made the Orange and Alexandria Railroad the only practical supply line from Washington, and any move that Lee made against it could be disastrous.

A little after midnight on the morning of October 13, the Twentieth Maine was hastily routed out and told to get into full marching equipment. The rumor flew among the enlisted men that the Rebels had flanked their position and were headed north again. The Fifth Corps went plodding up the rail line in the dark, and after a long, hard march they bivouacked at Catlett's Station. By noon of the next day, they had reached Bristoe Station and stopped there to boil coffee and eat some rations. Then suddenly, without the faintest warning, they found themselves being attacked.

A shell burst so close to Ben's campfire that he dropped his cup and threw himself flat. As he scrambled up again, unhurt, he saw a line of hated gray uniforms through the smoke. They were coming out of the woods to the west and streaming across the fields toward the railroad.

This was no place to stand and fight. The Fifth Corps departed northward at a fast pace, and the Second Corps, coming up behind, took the Rebels in the flank at Bristoe Station and beat them off. Meanwhile, the officers of the Fifth Corps were feeling somewhat ashamed. They turned the troops around and marched them back toward the sound of battle, but by the time they arrived, the Confederates were in retreat. Evening came on. Without stopping to rest, the corps, including the Twentieth Maine, had to hurry north once more. When they got to Bull Run in the small hours of the next morning, they had been on their feet twice around the clock and had marched a total of thirty-two miles.

Even then there wasn't much rest. On the fifteenth they headed north again, camped briefly at Fairfax Court House, then were roused in the middle of the night to march back to Centreville.

After three more days of these back-and-forth tactics, mostly slogging through the rain, Ben and his comrades were both tired and exasperated. They had shuttled up and down the railroad till the right-of-way was a sea of churned mud and there wasn't a fence rail or any other kind of firewood within miles of the tracks.

Down the line, in the meantime, Lee's soldiers were busy tearing up the rails. When the Union Army finally began moving south in earnest, its progress was slowed by having to repair the roadbed and lay new ties and track.

It was the seventh of November when the Twentieth Maine reached the neighborhood of the Rappahannock River once more. There they found that Lee's Army of Northern Virginia was solidly entrenched on the north side of the river. It looked as if the Confederate general meant to keep the Northerners from making any more thrusts toward Richmond.

At Rappahannock Station there was a hill that commanded the approach down the Orange Railroad, and the high ground was well fortified with redoubts, artillery emplacements, and several regiments of Lee's tough infantry in lines of rifle pits. Not only that, but in front of the earthworks was a wide, deep ditch, half full of mud and water, and farther out the ground was covered by an abatis of stumps and brush. On the whole it was a discouraging sight.

As they marched down the railroad, the Sixth Corps was over on the right of the tracks and the Fifth Corps on the left. When they came in sight of Lee's fortifications, there was a pause while batteries of field guns were brought up. The cannon pounded the Rebel works for a while but seemed to accomplish very little. If a real dent was to be made, it was pretty obvious that the foot soldiers would have to do it.

By a quirk of fortune, Ben Everett at that moment found himself over on the right-hand side of the tracks. The railroad made a bend to the left, and Company B had been crowded across next to the Sixth Maine regiment, which was part of the Sixth Corps.

When the Sixth Maine and Fifth Wisconsin were ordered forward to try a charge, Captain Morrill decided his company should take part in the fight.

"Come on, boys!" he shouted. "Those are Maine men—friends of ours. Let's go in with them!"

They had a lot of confidence in their company commander, and if he thought it was their job to tackle the fortifications, they would do it. So all eighty of them got ready to move, alongside the Sixth Maine.

It was almost sunset. With fixed bayonets, the thin blue skirmish line plowed through the brush and stumps and wallowed across the ditch. They were under heavy fire all the way, with round shot and musket balls tearing up the ground around them.

Several men near Ben went down. He saw a huge Maine lumberjack named Ed Morrison thrown clear across a pile of rocks by a cannon ball that had ripped away his knapsack. The giant leaped to his feet in a towering rage and rushed ahead so fast that he was the first attacker to reach the earthworks. But Ben and a dozen others were close at his heels. Their charge had been so fierce that the riflemen in the pits were too rattled to shoot straight. And now suddenly the Maine men were over the parapets, stabbing and swinging clubbed muskets.

Ben flailed away with the butt of his rifle, using it as he might have used an ax. The Confederates gave way stubbornly, still fighting as best they could, but more and more Yankees were pouring over the parapet now, as the Fifth Wisconsin got into the fray. There were many shocking sights in that brief battle, but one stuck in Ben's memory a long time. A slightly built young lieutenant of artillery stayed bravely by his gun after all the men in his battery were down or running. He trained the gun on the next wave of Union troops and was in the act of pulling the lanyard when somebody shot him dead. As he lay there by his gun, Ben saw with horror that he was a mere child, not over thirteen or fourteen.

There were still a few rough moments after that, for some of the Confederates had fled to adjoining trenches and were pouring in an enfilading fire from both sides. The Maine and Wisconsin men got down where they wouldn't be exposed and held on. Then fresh troops from the Sixth Corps overran the fortifications, and what was left of the enemy retreated to the river.

Company B could be justly proud of its part in the fight. In all, the Yankees captured four field guns, seventeen hundred prisoners, several battle flags, and a bridge train. The Sixth Maine suffered well over a hundred casualties, but Company B, of the Twentieth, had only one man killed and seven wounded. A long time later Captain Walter Morrill would receive the Congressional Medal of Honor for the action in which he led his company that day.

For Ben Everett the heady feeling of victory was dulled by one sad happening. At the very end of the battle, when the Confederates were in full flight across the bridge, a long-range battery opened up from the other side of the river. A number of shells burst in the trenches, now held by Yankee troops, and a fragment caught Loring Hawkes in the leg. The tow-headed farm boy was very pale when Ben reached him, and a good deal of blood was still oozing from his torn trouser leg. With a handkerchief Ben tied a knot above the knee and twisted the tourniquet tight. Then he stayed beside his friend, giving him water from his canteen, until stretcher-bearers came hunting for wounded in the dark.

"Ben," the injured soldier pleaded, "I didn't know I was goin' to be in a fight, so I didn't write to my folks. Will you send 'em a letter if I die?"

"Hush!" Ben told him gruffly. "You ain't about to die. Worst can happen, you might lose a leg. Then you could go home a hero."

The wounded lad grinned ruefully. "Yep," he replied, "a one-legged hero. Can't do much plowin' or mowin' on crutches, though."

When Ben got permission to ask about his friend at the field hospital next day, it cheered him to learn that the surgeons had saved the leg. A bone was broken but could be set, and the flesh wound ought to heal without trouble. Loring

Hawkes, with any luck, would be fit for action again in a few months. Meanwhile, he would be sent back to Washington by train and do his recovering in one of the big hospitals there.

The weather worsened in the next few days. There was early snow that caught the Army unprepared, and several men in the Twentieth Maine caught pneumonia from sleeping on the ground without shelter.

Lee had moved south to make another stand behind the Rapidan River. Soon the Union Army followed, for Meade, it seemed, had a plan for driving the Confederates out of their new defenses. There was a creek called Mine Run that formed the right flank of the Rebel line. If Federal forces could be put across the Rapidan lower down, they might be able to work around the flank and take Lee from the rear.

Ben was in the flanking force. On the next to the last day of November, he found himself staring across the waters of Mine Run at the Confederate defenses. They looked anything but encouraging. The creek itself had patches of ice along its sides, and the farther bank was not only steep but covered by a tangled mass of briars. Then, higher up the hill, he could see the line of rifle pits and gun emplacements.

The Maine regiment started digging in on their side of the stream and gloomily awaited the order to attack. When they started to build cook fires, Rebel pickets began firing at them.

"Hey! What's the idea?" yelled Ike Bean.

"You started it," came the answer.

"Not us. We only just got here."

It developed from the conversation that pickets from the Second Corps had begun the firing the day before. As soon as both forces understood each other, the sniping stopped, and Yankees and Rebels alike built fires to keep off the cold.

The morning of the thirtieth arrived with a bitter wind, and as soon as it was daylight, they heard artillery fire. Most of them, including Ben, had a feeling they would be butchered as soon as they began the assault. Some wrote hasty letters home. Others pinned tags with their names and addresses inside their shirts.

After a while, however, the firing died down, and word was passed from man to man that General Warren, the corps commander, had called off the attack. On December 1 the Maine regiment was pulled out of the picket line, and the Fifth Corps began marching north once more. The snow and cold had shut down, and fighting was over for the year 1863. Back at Rappahannock Station, the Twentieth Maine took over the old Rebel entrenchments, built comfortable log huts, and went into winter quarters.

Now that Loring Hawkes was no longer one of their cabin-mates, they invited big Ed Morrison to share the hut. Ike Bean had known the giant lumberjack back on the Penobscot and vouched for him as a good soldier and a good comrade. When a heavy log had to be carried or any other hard work done, his size and strength made him a valuable addition to their little group. The only drawback was his appetite. Ben had never seen a man eat the way Morrison did, and when they went foraging for food, it was necessary to bring double the amount needed by other squads.

Nevertheless, Ben liked the big fellow. He was nearly always good-natured, rarely got drunk, and his bass voice rumbled in harmony when they sang.

With no fighting in prospect during those cold winter months, a small number of enlisted men were given two-week furloughs. Ben was one of the unlucky ones, since he had enlisted much later than others in the regiment. One or two men from Skowhegan got permission to make the trip

home, and Ben wrote a letter of Christmas greetings to his mother, which they promised to deliver.

Then, on the twenty-fourth of December, he received a box from home. Judging by its weight, he knew it must have cost a deal of money to send. Hastily, he pried off the lid and caught the delicious smell of winter apples—a whole bushel of them. They were firm and juicy and tempting, and each one was carefully wrapped in newspaper. Without delay, each of the four men in the hut began munching the fruit.

"Hey," Martin Preble advised, "save those pieces o' paper. I ain't read a scrap o' down-East news in months."

Ben found another parcel in the box—a Christmas gift from his mother. It contained three pairs of hand-knit wool socks and a little pocket-sized Bible, which he put in the breast pocket of his uniform jacket. It was a common belief among soldiers of both North and South that a Bible would turn bullets and thus protect the owner's heart.

Long after the apples were gone, the bits of crumpled newspaper were read and reread and passed from hand to hand. Even such items as the birth of twin calves to the Widow Pease's cow seemed to bring home nearer to the young men.

Ben wrote another letter, thanking his mother for the box and telling her how much the apples were appreciated.

"I aim to try to read a Bible chapter every day," he added. "And if you could see what I've been wearing on my feet, you'd know the socks will come in useful. Right now the weather is most as cold as Maine, so wool feels good. You can't tell from one day to another, though. Last week we had a thaw, and about all the ice went out of the river, and it was warm as spring. We're comfortable here, but just the same I'll be glad when real spring comes and we can get on with the war."

7

The Wilderness

The rest of the winter passed pleasantly enough. There was regular drill and picket duty, but plenty of time remained for reading, writing letters, playing cards, or just sitting around the fire.

The Twentieth Maine was back to more nearly normal strength now, for in addition to wounded men returning to duty, they had received about a hundred new recruits. Some of these, of course, were poor material—"barrel scrapings," as the veterans called them. But once they had been absorbed into company units, most of them began to shape up. In all, the regimental rolls listed over five hundred men, and four hundred or more were present for duty.

With Colonel Gilmore off in Washington, serving on a court-martial, Major Ellis Spear had taken command of the Maine regiment, and he was a popular choice for the job.

"He's a peaked-lookin' little feller," Ike Bean commented. "You might think a strong breeze'd blow him away. But when it comes to plain grit, there ain't many can match him."

The Army of the Potomac had a new commander, too. He was a far different kind of man from the dapper McClellan, the flamboyant Burnside, the bumbling Hooker, or the precise, studious Meade. His name was Ulysses S. Grant, and he had been winning some pretty important battles in the West.

Ben was somewhat disappointed the first time he saw him. The whole Fifth Corps was drawn up in review that day, and half a dozen generals with their aides and escorts came riding past at a walk. Grant sat his big horse well, but his uniform was faded, weather-beaten, wrinkled, and unbuttoned. A brown beard covered his chin and cheeks, and he was chewing on a cigar. If it hadn't been for the three stars he wore, Ben would have taken him for a country storekeeper or perhaps a cattle buyer.

"Well," Martin Preble muttered, after the cavalcade had passed, "mebbe a plain man's what we need. We'll find out if he's got any gumption when the fightin' starts."

Before the first of May, they knew the fighting wasn't far off. Actually they had been getting ready since early in April. By the middle of that month overcoats and other winter garments were sent back to Washington. Then all the sick were shipped north to hospitals, and the Army was stripped for action.

Ben had come through the winter in good physical shape. He got on a scale in the quartermaster's depot and discovered he weighed a respectable hundred and seventy-five in boots and uniform. He even relished the prospect of the coming campaign—the marching, fighting, and short rations. At last, a year after his first experience in the ranks, he felt he was a soldier.

They broke camp, crossed the Rappahannock, and marched southward along the railroad. A heavy storm on the afternoon and night of May 2 drove the men to cover, but the next day dawned bright. Forming columns again, they moved on to Culpeper Court House and camped there, not far from the Rapidan. Beyond the river they knew Lee's Army of Northern Virginia was waiting behind strong entrenchments.

Just about midnight, the Twentieth Maine was ordered out of its blankets and started marching east. Before daylight, they had reached Germanna Ford, some distance down the river from the Confederate fortifications.

"I reckon Grant's gettin' ready to flank 'em," Ike Bean suggested. "If we go around their line an' git between them an' Richmond, Lee's bound to fight."

On that beautiful spring morning, they crossed the pontoon bridges laid by the engineers, and by midafternoon they came to a crossroads where thick woods grew all around a clearing.

The forest didn't look much like those in Maine. There were dense stands of scrubby second-growth pine—southern pine, quite different from the white pine they knew. And oak trees, dogwood, and sassafras grew among the evergreens. In addition, the undergrowth was a mass of brambles and vines.

"Pretty miserable kind o' place, ain't it?" Ed Morrison remarked. "Must be what they call the Wilderness."

Just how miserable it was they would soon find out. That night there were twenty-five thousand Federal soldiers in bivouac along the forest roads and in the few clearings. The air was balmy enough, but after the troops had settled down, the stillness of the woods made Ben shiver. All he heard was the hooting of an owl and the bark of a fox somewhere far away.

The Fifth Corps' First Division had been sent a mile or so west to guard the Orange Turnpike, and the Twentieth Maine was one of the regiments camped nearest to the enemy lines. They were wakened very early in the morning by the arrival of a message from the pickets. Rebel infantry was coming along the pike in considerable force.

The bulk of the Fifth Corps was supposed to march south at dawn, and its general decided the Confederate advance was no more than a demonstration by skirmishers. So all the rest of the troops started marching off, and the First Division was left alone to hold the road. Hardly had the men of Company B lighted their breakfast fires, when they were told to get themselves entrenched. They dug in willingly, chopped down trees to make breastworks, and cut away the brush for fifty yards in front to give them a field of fire. Then they came back to wait for developments.

The veterans knew they would be able to fight better on a full stomach, so coffee was soon boiling and hardtack being eaten. After that, there was nothing to do but sit tight. Ben looked around him at his comrades and noticed how various men reacted. Those without much imagination laughed and joked or went to sleep. But the best men in the regiment appeared quiet and thoughtful. Some of them might be dead before nightfall, and they were willing to face the fact soberly.

At last the waiting ended. General Griffin, in command of the Third Brigade, got his troops in battle formation. In the first line, to the left of the turnpike, facing west, were the Eighteenth Massachusetts and the Eighty-third Pennsylvania. Behind them the Corn Exchange Regiment, from Philadelphia, formed up beside the Twentieth Maine. All alone on the right side of the road was the Forty-fourth New York. And on the pike itself two pieces of artillery were wheeled into position. Though nothing was yet to be seen of the enemy, these guns started firing toward the west.

At the order the brigade started forward, and within minutes it was in the woods, floundering over fallen trees, forcing a path through the underbrush. So thick was the forest that Ben could see nothing of the Pennsylvania regiment ahead and caught only occasional glimpses of the men to his right and left.

"Keep that line closed up!" he heard Sergeant Gray shout. "Stay within ten feet of each other or you'll get lost!"

The heat was heavy in the woods, and only a light spring breeze stirred the young leaves overhead. Soon a snapping sound came from somewhere forward. A twig fell on Ben's arm, and he looked up to see leaves and small branches dropping as Rebel bullets cut them off. He was sweaty and panting, but he plowed on through the brush at the best pace he could make.

After a while he could see daylight between the trees, and Company B came stumbling out into a clearing. It looked about a quarter of a mile across—a field where corn had grown the year before. Out in the middle was the Eighty-third Pennsylvania, catching a lot of fire from the Confederates in the woods on the other side. The musketry made a steady, crackling roar, and the whole enemy line seemed to be one sheet of red flame.

"Come on!" Gray yelled to his platoon. "Hold your fire till we git right up to 'em!"

Then the blue line was crossing the field at a run, flattening the dead cornstalks and kicking up clouds of dust. They ran right through the halted Pennsylvanians and hit the crouching Rebels at the edge of the woods, firing at point-blank range as they approached. All the way across the cleared ground, they had been yelling at the top of their lungs.

Ben didn't know why he yelled, but it seemed to help. After a moment of bitter hand-to-hand fighting the gray line broke. Then it became a matter of driving them, hard on their heels, through the tangled brush. And as he ran, Ben suddenly caught the pungent reek of wood smoke. The forest in front of him was on fire.

Doggedly he and his companions kept up the pursuit. The smoke grew thicker as they went, and they could see little tongues of flame licking at the dry pine needles on the ground. Coughing and gasping, they stumbled out into a new and smaller clearing, where they had a better view of the retreating Confederates. Ben had reloaded his rifle. He was just taking aim when a sudden volley of musketry came from his right.

"My gosh!" Ike Bean called. "There's a whole mess o' Rebs over on the pike. We're bein' flanked!"

Captain Morrill ordered Company B into position facing the road, and they were soon returning the enemy's fire. But after two or three minutes it was obvious that they were far outnumbered. Gray uniforms kept coming down the road and slipping into the woods in their rear. If they were to avoid capture, they had to get back to the Union lines.

When the order to retreat came, they didn't turn and run. Keeping some semblance of a battle line, they moved back across the clearing, firing when they saw a chance. As they neared the shelter of the eastern woods, Ben was just reloading his rifle when something hit him in the head. He felt a moment's searing pain, felt himself falling forward, and then in an instant everything went black.

*   *   *

The first thing he was aware of, when he regained his senses, was a grunting sound. He was being carried like a sack of grain over somebody's shoulder. But he still clutched his rifle. The uniform close to his eyes was a faded blue. That made him feel better, for his first thought was that he had been taken prisoner.

"Hey," he muttered. "Put me down. I can make it on my own feet."

"Shut up!" a voice whispered. "We ain't through their lines yet!"

The back of the man carrying him was broad, and the long legs, seen from above, looked like tree trunks. They could belong to only one soldier in the company—big Ed Morrison. As his head cleared, Ben was conscious of a throbbing in his temple and a feeling of something wet dripping down his face. It was thick and red. He must be bleeding pretty freely.

A cloud of smoke engulfed them, and he strangled a cough. Then he realized that the woods all around them were afire. A badly wounded man would have no chance in those flames, and there must be a lot of wounded.

"Set me down," he told Morrison again. "I can walk. See if you can find somebody else that's hurt worse'n me."

This time the giant eased him down, and though his knees felt wobbly, he managed to walk fairly steadily.

"All right, boy," said Morrison. "Jest foller me, an' I'll look around."

A few yards farther on the big lumberjack came on a Yankee soldier from the Eighty-third Pennsylvania. He was helpless, shot through the hips. Morrison picked him up and trudged forward through the smoky woods, with Ben coming after as best he could.

It was growing dusk when they finally reached the lines of trenches they had dug that morning. The Twentieth Maine was there—or most of it—along with the rest of the Third Brigade. They were well dug in behind breastworks, and supper fires were going. Sergeant Gray came over to meet them.

"Well, sonny," he told Ben, "I thought we'd lost you for

sure. All you've got seems to be a crease. Minié ball must ha' grazed your head an' knocked you out. Bleedin' seems to be about stopped. Here—let me tie a bandage on, an' you'll be all right. Morrison, you've done a day's work. We'll take that wounded man off your hands an' send him back to the hospital."

Ben was starting to gulp down a cup of coffee when there was a stir in the lines. Lieutenant Melcher, of Company F, arrived with some eighteen men of his command.

"Where you been?" Gray asked a corporal in the group.

"Us? Why, we *fought* our way back with the bayonet," the soldier replied proudly. "Brung in thirty-two prisoners to prove it. Reckon B Company's got a ways to go to match that!"

Ben hadn't lost as much blood as he thought. He felt a bit tired and the scalp wound smarted, but at least he wasn't a hospital case. As soon as he had eaten some of Preble's "stew," made with salt pork and hardtack and served piping hot, he began to feel better.

There was little sleeping done that night, for the fire in the woods still smoldered and the smoke lay like a pall over the lines. They shivered when they heard the distant cries of wounded men, lost out there among the creeping flames. Occasional bursts of nervous firing came from the skirmishers, who couldn't see what they shot at. About the only advantage brought by the smoke was the absence of mosquitoes.

The first day in the Wilderness had been hard on the First Division. The Maine regiment had eleven killed and seventy wounded or missing, and it had gone even worse with some of the other units. But that wasn't the only reason morale was low among the men behind the breastworks. They had had strong hopes of General Grant's leadership, and the first battle was certainly no victory.

"Know what we'll do next?" Ike Bean asked glumly. "Same as all the other times—pull back acrost the Rapidan an' mebbe the Rappahannock."

The following day, May 6, passed in comparative quiet. Along toward night the Sixth Corps, which was over on their right, retreated in disorder after a sharp Rebel attack. The Maine men were afraid they would be flanked again, but they hung on, with the rest of the brigade, and before dark the Sixth Corps retook its positions.

On the seventh the air was thick with fog and smoke, and the sickening odor of gunpowder fumes and burned flesh hung heavy over the lines. It was barely daylight when a body of Confederates came yelling through the mist, broke up the squads on picket duty, and was almost into the earthworks before the Twentieth Maine drove them back.

Later the firing lightened somewhat. Back at the rear, the Army of the Potomac was starting to pull out, just as Ike Bean had foretold. And four or five regiments, including the Maine men, were given the job of covering the Fifth Corps' withdrawal.

Colonel Herring, of the Corn Exchange Regiment, was left in command. He moved along the lines and encouraged the men.

"No use sitting still," he said. "We'll hit 'em. Hit 'em so hard they won't have time to guess how few of us are left."

The Twentieth Maine and the Sixteenth Michigan led the attack. Enemy pickets were out in some force, but the Yankees crumpled them up and drove them a quarter of a mile, right up to the Rebel breastworks. When the artillery fire got too heavy, they pulled back about halfway and dug in once more.

At dusk Ben heard a yelling from the Confederate line. It sounded as if a new attack was starting. Then he realized that the yells came from farther and farther away. The Army of Northern Virginia must be moving back, just as the main force of the Federals was.

The weary soldiers lay there with loaded rifles all night, and in the morning the woods in front of them were empty. Then an aide rode up to tell Colonel Herring he could pull his men out, and ten minutes later the little brigade was buzzing with news. The Union Army wasn't retreating to the Rapidan. It was heading south, down the road to Spotsylvania Court House!

"Mebbe this feller Grant's the kind o' general we've been lookin' for, after all," said Ben Everett.

Spotsylvania

Colonel Herring's picket brigade set out before daylight to follow the rest of the Army southward. It was hot, the air still thick with smoke, mixed with the great clouds of dust raised by the thousands of marching men ahead. And the Twentieth Maine, after three sleepless days and nights, was nearly ready to drop. Ben felt about as fit as any of them, which wasn't saying much. The big bandage around his head had been exchanged for a pad of gauze held on by sticking plaster. The wound no longer hurt except for some itching as it healed, and he was able to wear his cap once more.

By ten o'clock they could hear heavy gunfire off to the south, and before long they could catch glimpses of the battle in progress. Lee, it seemed, had guessed what Grant was doing and had won the race to Spotsylvania Court House.

The men of the Twentieth Maine had now been separated from their own Third Brigade for twenty-four hours, and they were anxious to get back there. But the Third was fighting somewhere else, and it was decided that the mixed troops under Herring should stay together and fight under General Crawford, of the Third Division.

Hungry, tired, and exasperated, the Maine men set out with the Third Division about sundown to attack a wooded crest called Laurel Hill. When the other brigades went forward, they were kept in the rear as a supporting line. Around them were scattered clumps of pine and cedar, and in the darkness it was hard to see any distance.

All of a sudden they stumbled onto the front line of Union troops, which had halted to fire. From very close there came a great burst of answering shots, and then the Rebels were on them, yelling as they ran. It all happened so fast that by the time the Confederates reached Ben's company, the bulk of General Crawford's troops had left for the rear.

"Hang on, boys—they can't drive us!" one of their officers shouted. And the Maine men, after falling back a few yards, rallied in a charge of their own. The rest of the little picket brigade fought staunchly at their side.

Ben didn't feel brave. He just felt mad. With no time to reload his rifle, he clubbed it and heard the gratifying *thunk* as it landed on an enemy's head. Then he was wrestling, body to body, with a wiry Confederate about his own size. By luck he tripped him, but his opponent squirmed quickly out and pinned the Maine boy's shoulders. Ben saw the flash of a knife and had the ghastly feeling that it was all over. His life was saved by young Lieutenant Melcher of Company F, who cut the Rebel down with his sword.

That was the kind of fight it was, bloody and brutal. After a while the men in gray must have thought they were battling a whole division, instead of the six or seven hundred men actually involved. The fighting died down, and the victorious Yankees stood there panting in the dark while the enemy pulled back.

Even though the Twentieth Maine had taken nearly a hundred prisoners, it had been a costly battle. Twenty-three of their own enlisted men were wounded or killed, and they had lost three company officers. What they should do next was a question nobody seemed able to answer. Colonel Herring sent a succession of messengers to division head-quarters for orders, and when they finally returned, they had permission for the brigade to pull back. It was three in the morning when the Maine men picked up their dead and wounded and toiled down the slope of Laurel Hill to the rear.

At last Ben was heading back toward bivouac and a chance to rest. It was as black a night as he had ever seen. Helping one of his comrades who had suffered a head wound, he stumbled with him through the woods, unable to see more than a few feet ahead. Suddenly, without warning, there was a musket flash almost in their faces. Ben felt a sear-ing pain in the thigh of his left leg and pitched forward on his hands and knees, angrier than he had ever been in his life.

"You durn fool!" he yelled. "We're friends—Twentieth Maine! Ain't you ever been on picket duty before?"

The man who had fired was another New Englander from a Massachusetts regiment. Shaken, he stammered an apology and called back for help. Soon a pair of stretcher-bearers appeared and carried Ben to the rear, while the other Maine man walked beside them.

The leg was bleeding a good deal. Still lying on the stretcher, Ben took off his belt and bound it tightly above the wound, hoping to stop the flow. It helped somewhat, but he felt lightheaded by the time they arrived at the dress-ing station. A surgeon, gray-faced with weariness, ripped away the young soldier's pants leg and examined the wound.

"How's it feel?" he asked. "Much pain?"

"At first there was," Ben replied drowsily. "Mostly just sort o' numb now."

"Well," the doctor told him, "you're more fortunate than some. The bullet went clear through and never touched the bone. If you can keep it clean, you won't lose the leg. Just a couple o' weeks in the hospital and you'll be ready to march again. First, though, we've got to stop the bleeding."

"Thanks," Ben muttered, and dropped off to sleep.

He was blissfully unconscious of the probing and bandaging. When he woke up, it was early morning, and Martin Preble was there with a cup of hot soup. His thigh felt stiff but gave him no great pain.

"Pretty lucky, you are!" Preble grinned. "Goin' back to a clean bed an' mebbe a nice young nurse! We'll try an' hold the regiment together till you're fit to fight again."

Shortly after Martin left, a battered Army supply wagon backed up to the dressing station, and the orderlies started loading in the wounded. Ben was one of six men lying on the wagon bed. There was a little straw, but it was filthy with dirt and stale blood, and unlike the regular ambulance wagons, this one had no springs.

"How far are they takin' us?" asked a young New York soldier with one arm shot away.

"Fredericksburg," the orderly replied curtly. Afterward, Ben was sure the man must have known the misery in store for them on that ride.

As the crow flies, it was only a dozen miles to Fredericksburg, but the roads were twisting and rough and the horses slow. It was hot, too, and the steady jolting was almost unbearable for the more seriously wounded men. They screamed or sobbed their anguish, and when the bandages worked loose, their bleeding started again. Ben did what he could to retie their dressings, but he was suffering a good deal himself. On and on the wagons crawled, fording streams, bumping over rocks. It was late that night when the little train of four or five wagons reached the half-ruined town on the Rappahannock.

Fredericksburg had never recovered from the shelling by Union artillery under Burnside, and the citizens, with few comforts themselves, had little kindness to spare for Yankees. So the wounded were put in vacant stores, or warehouses, or even in alleys. There were thousands of them after the bloody fighting in the Wilderness, and surgeons, beds, and medicines were in such short supply that many men died before they could get proper attention.

Ben was one of the lucky ones. He got a blanket to lie on and was quartered with some seventy others in an empty hardware store. Part of the roof was gone, and it leaked badly when it rained. The food was regular Army rations, brought in once or twice a day. As for pretty nurses, the nearest Ben came to seeing one was when a fat, middle-aged lady from the Sanitary Commission visited their makeshift hospital. All she did was moan at the misery around her and wring her hands.

It was something of a miracle that Ben's wound healed at all. Men within a few yards of him developed gangrene, and their swollen, blackened limbs had to be taken off. Even so, one of them died the next day. But after a week in the place, a surgeon told Ben with some surprise that he could get up and walk a little if he liked.

Three days later he was discharged by the medical officers and told he could rejoin his unit. He could have ridden one of the wagons going back for more wounded, but after his experience he preferred to make the journey on foot. With a blanket, a full canteen, and a knapsack containing a little food, he started south along the Richmond Railroad line on the twenty-first of May.

The Army of the Potomac, he had heard, was swinging

southeast again after Spotsylvania, and he hoped to catch up with the rear guard after a day's marching. He carried his uniform jacket, and in Fredericksburg he had been given a pair of trousers formerly owned by a soldier who had died. They were faded and ragged but fitted him reasonably well.

It was a hot day. He didn't try to go very fast but limped steadily down the dusty railroad bed. Every half mile or so he would be challenged by guards protecting the track and the telegraph line, and they confirmed the fact that the Federal Army was somewhere in front of him.

"You'll likely catch 'em at one o' the fords," a corporal told him. "They's a lot o' little rivers to cross, all flowin' into the Mattapony."

Twice he rested, ate a little, and then pushed on. By dusk he figured he had come about ten miles. The wounded leg stiffened a little while he slept, but he refused to let it slow him down. After a mile or so, that second morning, he got over the stiffness and hiked on with less difficulty.

The line of the railroad had made a bend to the left, but he could see the Mattapony River below and was certain he would come to a crossing soon. A couple of miles farther on, the track swung south again and he found himself on a trestle over the river. Luckily no train came until he was safely across. And almost as soon as he reached the farther bank, he saw a widespread cloud of dust ahead. It could only be the rear columns of the Union Army.

Ben walked faster then. At the next picket post he asked for the whereabouts of the First Division of the Fifth Corps. The soldiers had no idea.

"If you want to find 'em," they told him, "just keep a-goin'. The Army's spread out over half o' Virginny, but your outfit's sure to be up ahead somewhere."

It was past noon before Ben got the information he needed. A sergeant led him to one of the divisional head-quarters tents, and after a wait he was allowed to talk to the adjutant.

"Hm, Twentieth Maine, eh?" said the officer. "That's in the Third Brigade, First Division, Fifth Corps. Just now I believe your brigade's leading the advance somewhere on the right. Where's your rifle?"

"I left it behind, sir, at the dressing station, after the fight at Laurel Hill. That's where I got wounded."

"And you've been in a hospital at Fredericksburg? How'd you get here?"

"I walked, sir."

"Well," said the adjutant, "it might be a good thing if we had a few more like you. I'll see that you get a rifle and am-munition. Good luck, soldier."

To his delight, Ben was issued a brand-new Springfield. It was as effective as the familiar Enfield and easier to keep in order. With the weapon under his arm, he set off once more for the front.

Sunset came, and then darkness. Though he had passed many regimental bivouacs and heard occasional firing in the distance, he still had no clue to the location of the Twentieth Maine. He was in a little patch of woods and had just decided to camp there when the dim evening light disclosed another soldier only a few yards away. The man was stooping to pick up a stick of firewood, and Ben couldn't make out the color of his uniform.

"Halt!" he growled. "Who goes there?"

The man stood up, startled, and Ben saw he was unarmed. Moreover the squat, broad-shouldered figure looked famil-iar.

"Ike!" he cried. "Good thing I didn't shoot! First off I took you for a Reb skirmisher. You camped somewhere close?"

"I'll be dum-swizzled!" Bean replied. "If 'tain't Ben Everett in the flesh! Come on, boy—the reg'ment's right over beyond them trees. Sure didn't expect to see you fer a spell."

Company B received him back with open arms. They were tired, having fought a fairly stiff engagement at a place called Pole Cat Creek that day. But after they had fed him, his squadmates sat up long enough to hear Ben's account of conditions in Fredericksburg and his lonely hike of the past two days.

"When they took you off in that meat wagon," Ed Morrison admitted, "I figured we'd prob'ly never see you again. At the best, it looked like that leg'd have to come off. You must be a healthy cuss, Ben."

He slept soundly that night and turned out for roll call with the rest in the morning. Major Spear, in command of the regiment, came over personally to congratulate him on his safe return. Then, as soon as a hasty breakfast was eaten, the column formed to march south with the rest of the brigade.

Toward noonday they reached the North Anna River and made their crossing at Jericho Ford. As they waded, knee-deep, shots began to fly from the farther side. Ben ducked his head and kept on with his company, not stopping to fire till he reached the shelter of the bank. Then they were all scrambling up, meeting the Confederates at the top and throwing them back. It was a loud, brisk little battle while it lasted, and several Maine men were wounded. One of them was Major Spear, but his wound was slight, and after having it dressed, he came back to take charge of his command.

They rested a short time, then pushed on after the Rebels.

It was rough country, partly wooded and full of swamps and small streams, so their advance was slow. On the twenty-sixth, in the middle of the night, they were ordered back across the North Anna once more, in one of those swings to the left flank that was typical of Grant's strategy.

Some of the Maine men, short on sleep, grumbled at being routed from their blankets. "Durn it," said Ike Bean, "'pears to me we ain't supposed to do a thing but fight all day an' march all night!"

"Well," Ben told him, "I'd rather do that than be back in that blame store they called a hospital."

The Chickahominy

The Army of the Potomac still wheeled southeastward. They were drawing closer to Richmond with each advance, but always General Lee was there in front, his forces well dug in.

Ben's regiment crossed the Pamunkey River on May 28 and immediately ran into strong Rebel troops. It was becoming second nature to the Yankee veterans to build breastworks wherever they met resistance. No shovels were provided, but they used what they had—bayonets, tin plates, knives, and sticks. In ten minutes of hard work, they dug themselves shallow trenches with little earthworks in front to give them some protection from rifle fire.

With the marching, the digging, the night patrols and frequent skirmishes, none of them ever seemed to get enough sleep. And for a month they had nothing to eat but coffee and hardtack, varied by an occasional bit of stringy beef from a starved stray cow.

By early June they were in the swampy country north of the Chickahominy River. The woods were full of bog holes, and the standing water bred mosquitoes by the millions. Marching was almost impossible except on the few roads, and those were strongly held by the Confederates.

On June 3 there was a big attack by the Union Army at

Cold Harbor—a strange name indeed, for the place was far from the seacoast and it was stifling hot. The Twentieth Maine was on the right of the line, so their battle was a short distance north, at Bethesda Church. There was a lot of hard fighting, and as far as Ben could see, it gained them nothing. The regiment lost twenty-six men, killed or wounded.

After that they were shifted southeast again, floundering still deeper into the swamps. The sun was hot and the air sultry in the daytime. And night or day, when the wind was from the northwest, the smell of unburied soldiers and dead horses left at Cold Harbor was enough to turn a strong man's stomach.

Two or three nights after the battle, Ben's platoon was sent out on picket duty. There was no moon, and the little handful of men had to spread out too far to see each other. The only noises were an occasional snapping twig and the eerie calls of owls and whippoorwills. Ben shivered with lonesomeness. He clutched his Springfield and listened intently for any possible enemy movement.

Off to his left, he heard a stealthy sound of splashing. Cautiously he started in that direction and suddenly felt the ground drop out from under him. A moment later he was struggling to free his legs from the bottomless slime of a boghole. He didn't dare call for help. If the noise he had heard was made by a Rebel, he would almost certainly be captured.

Then a voice challenged sharply. "Hey! Who's there?"

He knew from the accent it was a Maine man speaking. "It's me—Everett," he answered. "I'm stuck in the swamp. Give me a hand if you can, but be careful where you step."

Out of the gloom a shape appeared, and a rifle muzzle was thrust within his reach. He gripped it with all his strength and was able at last to pull a foot free. When he stood on solid ground again, he took a closer look at his deliverer. It was Martin Preble, and he was doubled over with silent laughter.

"Durn if you didn't sound like a bogged-down cow, the way your feet was suckin' in the mud." Preble snickered. "Wonder what time it's gittin' to be. Seems as if we'd oughter be relieved pretty soon."

Ben wasn't the only soldier who stumbled into the mire during that time in the Chickahominy swamps. There was a man in Company E who lost both his boots and had to go barefoot for weeks. And in a more serious case, a young recruit went out on patrol one night and was never seen again. Some thought he had deserted or been taken prisoner, but most of the regiment blamed the treacherous quicksand in the bogs.

It was a relief to the Twentieth Maine when orders came to march eastward again. The brigade moved out with some secrecy and headed for a ford a few miles down the Chickahominy. The march was made at night. Before dawn they were over the river, and the main part of the Union forces continued south toward the James. Grant's new idea, so the rumor went among the enlisted men, was to bypass Richmond, where Lee was so strongly entrenched, and move against Petersburg.

Ben didn't go with them, however. He had barely had time to eat breakfast when some units of his brigade were ordered westward. They were evidently part of a covering force, whose job was to screen the withdrawal of the rest of the Army.

"We're likely to run into enemy patrols any time," Major Spear told his men. "So we need a skirmish line out in front. You don't have to keep too quiet. What we want is to make 'em think this is a big attack, with lots of troops."

The detachment marched half a dozen miles, staying in the woods for the most part. About eleven they stopped to rest and had some hardtack, along with water from their canteens. Then Company B was told to take over the skirmishers' job. So far not a Rebel had been seen, and Ben began to wonder, as he moved out ahead of the regiment, whether they would go all the way to Richmond without a fight.

The skirmish line was thin. Only once in a while did he catch a glimpse of the men on either side of him, prowling forward through the thickets. To the north the Chickahominy must make a bend in their direction, for he thought he could see a dim glint of water over there.

"Ed," he called in a low voice. "Ed Morrison—you reckon that's the river, there to the right?"

There was no answer from the big soldier, and Ben decided he must be too far away to hear. He resettled his knapsack and cartridge box and went on. But before he had taken three steps, a man rose up suddenly in front of him. It was a lean, bearded Confederate soldier with a rifle pointed squarely at his chest.

"Come quiet, Yank," whispered the Rebel. "Drop yo' gun an' put yo' hands up, 'less'n you want to die."

The man wore blue Union pants and a butternut shirt, faded to a kind of gray. He looked like a scarecrow, but there was a deadly intention in his hard, cold eyes. Ben dropped his rifle and threw his hands up. He still half expected to be shot.

"Move," said the implacable voice. "Come past me, an' start walkin'."

So this, thought the young New Englander, was what it felt like to be taken prisoner. He moved mechanically past the shallow trench where the man had lain hidden, then on through the woods, with the Rebel's rifle muzzle a yard from

his shoulder blades. It seemed like a long distance but was probably no more than half a mile before they reached a larger line of trenches, manned by a company of gray-clad infantry. The men lay there with their muskets ready on the earthworks, but a sergeant stood up as Ben and his captor approached.

"See ye got one, Zeke," remarked the noncom. "That's the second Yank you boys have brung in."

Zeke grinned and spat tobacco juice over the embankment. "This un's tall enough," he replied, "but scarce wuth keepin'. Ain't much more'n a shirttail young'un. Save his boots fer me, will yuh?"

"Leave him here an' git back to picketin'," the sergeant ordered. "Yeah, you kin have his boots. Too big fer me. I'll take him to the cunnel, an' we'll find out if'n he kin talk."

Ben was led barefoot back to the regimental headquarters behind the lines. The "cunnel" turned out to be a fussy little man with sweeping gray whiskers. He kept the young prisoner standing for several minutes while he fiddled with papers on his camp table. At last he was ready to question him.

"Well," he barked, "what's yo' name?"

"Benjamin Everett."

"Say *sir,* you lout! Or don't they teach you that in the Yankee Army?"

"Yes, sir," Ben replied.

"How old are you?"

"Seventeen, sir."

"Rank—obviously a private. What's yo' regiment?"

"Twentieth Maine." It slipped out before Ben remembered he wasn't required to tell.

"What brigade—what division?"

"I can't say, sir. We've been on detached service."

"Well—where's the rest o' the Union Army?"

"I don't know, sir."

The colonel's face got red. "Don't know, eh? Or won't tell—which?"

"Both, sir. I couldn't tell if I did know, but I don't."

The officer fumed and cursed. "All right," he said. "Take off that jacket and give it to my orderly. We can use good clothes, even if they're blue."

Ben obeyed reluctantly but took the little book from the inside breast pocket. "May I keep this Bible, sir?" he asked. "It's a present from my mother."

"Hrrumph!" snorted the colonel. "I suppose you may. Nothin' dangerous about the Gospels."

Outside the headquarters tent, Ben saw a familiar face. "Rocky" Joe Sampson was a granite cutter from Hallowell, Maine, and a member of Company B. Now he stood there under guard, his powerful shoulders drooping dejectedly. They had no chance then to speak to each other, for three Confederate soldiers were waiting to march them off.

Ben was bone-tired and low in spirits. As he soon saw, any attempt to make a break would be hopeless. His hands were tied behind him, and the little procession set off. One soldier led the way, then came the two prisoners in single file, and two more armed men brought up the rear.

After a quarter of a mile, they were in the woods again, moving steadily westward, the afternoon sun in their faces. A born woodsman, Ben began studying landmarks as they went. If he should ever come this way again, he would re-member the lay of the land.

Once or twice he got close enough to Sampson to speak a few words. "Where you think they're takin' us?" he asked in a low voice.

"Dunno. Richmond, most likely. They've got prisons there."

"Shut up, y'all, an' keep movin'," ordered a guard behind them.

Two or three miles farther on, they swung to the left and came out into more open country. There were several big farms—plantations, Ben supposed they were called. Handsome brick houses with white columns sat back among the trees. In the fields, he saw Negroes working in the rows of tobacco.

Then, a short time later, they came in sight of a broad river. Ben had never seen the James, but he was sure this must be it. The water was close to a mile wide at that point, and from the direction of the sun, he could tell that the river was flowing south. They came out on a road, not far from the bank, and followed it northward.

It wasn't long before distant steeples came into view beyond a bend in the river. There were many of them. It must be a big town, and Ben was certain now that they were heading for the capital of the Confederate States.

Richmond, in the late afternoon sun of early June, looked serene and peaceful. It wasn't until they reached the outer fortifications and saw hundreds of gray-uniformed troops that the first impression changed. This was a city at war. Soldiers were everywhere, and orderlies on fast horses raced hither and thither, throwing up clouds of dust. The long lines of tents showed where many regiments must be quartered.

The hot four-hour march had tired Ben's leg, and he was limping a little when they entered the city itself. But his eyes were still alert. Across the river he could see that there was no military encampment close to the bank. Instead, the shore on both sides was lined with dingy warehouses, factories, and occasional docks. Off to the right the streets climbed upward toward rounded hills, each of them crowned by impressive-looking homes and public buildings. There were several bridges crossing the James. The first one they came to was a wagon bridge over which a good deal of traffic was moving. Above, two railroad trestles spanned the wide expanse of river. And between them Ben could see a series of rapids, where the water came tumbling down, white and foaming.

Soon after they passed the second railroad bridge, a long black steel mill could be seen near the river on their left. From it came a clang of steam hammers, and the smoke rising from its tall chimneys gave an appearance of furious activity. Not till afterward did Ben learn that this was the famous Tredegar Iron Works, one of the principal arsenals of the South.

Once beyond the big factory, they were close to the waterfront, a canal on their right and the river on their left.

"All right, Yanks," announced one of their guards, "here we are. Yonder's Belle Isle Prison."

They looked out across half a mile of water to a low island in the middle of the river. It was more than a mile long, Ben judged, and roughly half as wide. It must have been a pretty place once, with trees and grass—perhaps a picnic ground for the people of Richmond. Now, even from that distance, he could see that it swarmed with men like an anthill.

There was a small steam ferryboat docked opposite the island. Other guards, with other prisoners, appeared shortly, and they were marched aboard the craft. There was more waiting then, but after a while the whistle tooted and they pulled out into the river. Looking over the side, Ben noticed how fast the water flowed as it swept down toward the falls.

The boat had to head upstream and approach the island crab-fashion to compensate for the rushing current.

Sampson and Ben were standing close together amidships when they heard an altercation going on a little way forward. A peevish voice was complaining loudly.

"I tell you I ain't a prisoner—not by rights! All I was tryin' to do was desert from the stinkin' Yankee Army an' join up with you folks!"

Ben thought he knew that voice and craned his neck to see. To his disgust he recognized his old traveling companion, Perley Snell. It was about what he might have expected from a would-be bounty-jumper and confirmed malingerer. The guards, however, merely laughed at him.

"You mis'able houn'," one of them told him roughly. "That's the oldes' dodge in the war! Half the pris'ners we take claim to be on our side. So jes' hesh yo' mouth. We wouldn't have a polecat like you fightin' fer us, nohow."

The ferry was nosing into its slip on the shore of the island. There was a high stockade surrounding the landing, and sentry boxes mounted on either side frowned down forbiddingly on the prisoners as they were marched up the gangplank.

"Yere we are!" the captain of the boat sang out. "You are now on bee-utiful Belle Isle. An' yo' tickets don't entitle you to no return trips!"

10

Belle Isle

A heavy gate opened in the stockade, and a double file of uniformed Confederates came out to take over the eight new prisoners. There followed a few minutes of joshing between the soldiers who had brought them from the front and the prison guards. Apparently, men who fought in the lines had a low opinion of such work.

Then the ferry whistle sounded, and the soldiers went back on board. With their hands still bound, Ben, Sampson, and the rest were prodded along through the entrance and the gate closed behind them with a clang. The moment they were inside, a loud shouting arose all around them. Hundreds of ragged prisoners came hurrying forward.

"Fresh fish! Fresh fish!" they were yelling.

Then a guard untied Ben's hands and pushed him into the midst of the throng. At once the prisoners were crowding against him, feeling his pockets, grabbing at his shirt. They were no better than animals, he was shocked to realize. Angrily he elbowed them away, but not before one big, ugly-looking bruiser had snatched his precious Bible. Ben made a lunge for it and was promptly given such a shove that he fell over backward.

From the ground he saw Rocky Sampson come plowing

through the mass of onlookers. The stonecutter sent men spinning to right and left till he reached the fellow who had taken the Bible.

"Give it here," he growled. "That boy's a friend o' mine."

"Oh-ho!" cried the bully with a leer. "Ye're talkin' to Black Dan McKenna now, me buck. The best rough-an'-tumble fighter on the Bowery—that's me! An' here's me sap to prove it!"

From nowhere he produced a wicked-looking tube of leather, apparently weighted with shot or stones, and he slapped it against his palm with an ominous *thunk*. He was taller than the thick-set Maine man, and with his big paunch, he looked heavier.

Sampson faced him with no weapon but his own sledge-hammer fists. "All right," he said calmly, "if that's the way you want it, we'll fight for it."

He took a slow step forward, his eyes on the New York Irishman. McKenna shifted his feet and suddenly swung the blackjack with an expert hand. But Sampson's head wasn't there. He had side-stepped the blow and sprung forward with the same motion. One hand caught the bully's wrist, twisting it till he dropped the leather sap. The other fist came up in a short, jolting arc that landed on the point of the jaw. Lifted clean off the ground, McKenna went down with a crash and lay there without moving.

"Here y'are, Ben," said Sampson, picking up the Bible. "Now let's find ourselves a place to sleep."

The crowd of prisoners was impressed. They opened a wide path to let the two Maine men through, and some of them voiced their approval.

"A good job," one gaunt Yankee said. "I wish ye'd killed the dirty devil. He's been runnin' things too long 'round here."

Sampson turned to him. "Mebbe you can help us, friend," he suggested. "We're new to the place. What do folks do here for shelter? An' what about grub?"

The man shook his head. "Them as was lucky 'nough to have any blankets when they was took, gen'ally bed down on 'em. All the tents was used up long ago. What ye have to do is pick a likely place to lay down an' pray it don't rain. As fer rations—we git 'em once a day. In the mornin', that is, an' them with good stummicks manage to eat the stuff. All it is is corn bread an' sowbelly—now an' then a handful o' cowpeas."

They thanked him and walked on, looking the island over. Most of the high ground was solidly occupied. Many of the earlier prisoners had found wood, or at least brush, and had built themselves little shelters of a sort. Old tent canvas or ragged blankets formed the roofs of these shacks. The common name for them, Ben learned, was "shebangs."

They moved on, down to lower ground on the south side of the island. Here were the latrines—long ditches dug in the swampy earth. The stench from this area was more than they could stand, and they started looking elsewhere.

"Keerful, there!" one of the prisoners warned them. "You fellers was mighty close to the deadline a minute ago. Nothin' these lousy guards like better'n to shoot a man that gits over the line."

"Where is it?" Ben asked. "I don't see any marks."

"Oh, it ain't marked. But any time you're a hundred yards from the shore, you know that's too close. See them pickets marchin' back an' forth? They're carryin' loaded guns."

"Hm," said Sampson. "Don't look as if it'd be very easy to git away. Anybody tried it?"

The man grinned, showing toothless gums. He didn't

look old—thirty-five perhaps—but he was thin and bent, and his lips were swollen with scurvy.

"Some few have tried," he said, "but they was either shot in the water or else swep' over the falls an' drownded."

It was rapidly growing dark now, and since no better place could be found, Ben and his friend lay down on a patch of ground between two ramshackle shebangs.

"We're all right tonight," Sampson remarked. "Don't look like rain an' it's plenty warm. But we better git ourselves a poncho or a piece o' canvas 'fore the weather changes. Mebbe we could trade for 'em. You got any money?"

"A couple o' dollars," Ben whispered. "I sewed 'em in the waistband o' my pants. Got my jackknife, too, but that's all except the little Bible an' my sewin' kit."

"Well, we'll see what we can do in the mornin'." The big man yawned. "G'night, Ben."

*   *   *

The smoke of a nearby cook fire woke them at daylight. The whole island was stirring with slowly moving figures. More than ever it made Ben think of an anthill. The few lucky ones who had a little firewood were cooking messes that would pass for breakfast. Others went trailing down to the latrines. And many simply crawled about aimlessly, warming themselves in the morning sun. Their faces had a beaten, hopeless look, and their emaciated bodies were in rags.

Not all the prisoners were in such miserable shape, however. McKenna and his gang of toughs seemed to be better fed and better clothed than the rest. No doubt they had taken what they wanted by force. Later that morning the Maine men heard more about them. They called themselves "Black Dan's Spoilers," and there were enough of them to make themselves a terror to the unorganized prisoners. After what had happened yesterday, however, they left Sampson and Ben strictly alone.

Inside the stockade, near the ferry gate, were houses where the officers and guards were quartered and a small storehouse where the food was kept. At ten o'clock a rickety wagon came through the gate, and there was a rush of prisoners in that direction. They lined up in a double file so that the wagon could pass between them. And two guards tossed down the food. Each man got a chunk of corn pone and a small, greasy bit of rancid salt pork.

Ben had been pleased when he heard corn bread was issued, but he was bitterly disappointed in the piece he got. Instead of the tender, well-buttered corn bread he was used to at home, this stuff was coarse and tasteless, made with meal that had the cobs ground in along with the corn. The pork also gagged him, but he finally swallowed it, knowing he ought to keep up his strength.

There was no spring on Belle Isle. For water the prisoners went in single file to a spot on the bank at the upper end of the island, where they were allowed to drink or fill cans. The place was heavily guarded, of course, since it was the only break in the deadline.

Sampson did some trading that morning. He had a silver ring, which he swapped for a battered can that could be used for fetching water or boiling stew. And with one of Ben's dollars he purchased a square of old tent canvas, ragged and dirty but still serviceable. Money, it seemed, was in great demand. The guards would trade real food if they got United States currency in return.

Shortly after noon the prisoners had to line up for roll call. They formed into companies of a hundred men each and were not only counted but also had to answer to their names.

Ben and his companion had been assigned to the Twelfth Hundred, and they had to wait two hours in line while a corporal and two soldiers checked off all the names. If anybody was missing, a friend was expected to give the reason and tell where he could be found. A good many men were sick and unable to report for roll call that day. As soon as the hundred was dismissed, the guards went to ferret out the sick.

Outside of the military hospital in Fredericksburg, Ben had never seen so much sickness. At first he found it hard to understand, but after trying to eat the miserable rations, one reason at least was plain. He talked about it to a man from the Ninth Wisconsin who had stood next to him in the line.

"Most of 'em," the Westerner told him, "start off with dysentery. You eat that corncob bread long enough an' your bowels are bound to go bad. Then a lot more git scurvy because they ain't given any fresh vegetables—not even potatoes. Their gums go rotten an' their teeth fall out, an' they can't even stand up straight."

"Does it kill 'em?" Ben asked in horror.

"Sooner or later, sure. I reckon about ten men die every week here. There's a sort o' hospital down by the gate where they take the worst cases, but by that time the prisoners are goners, anyhow. Nobody ever comes back from there. You just come in? Where was you took?"

"Only about a dozen miles off, over yonder," Ben replied. "You've been here quite a spell, I judge."

The man nodded. "Since December. I was in Pappy Thomas's army when we beat the Rebs at Missionary Ridge. But I got hit on the head with a musket butt, an' when I come to, I was a prisoner. They shipped me east in a cattle car, an' there was a blizzard on the way. Lucky they let me keep my blanket or I wouldn't ha' come through the trip, let alone the rest o' the winter."

Rummaging around in a gully behind a pile of rocks, Ben found a few gnarled sticks of driftwood. How they had been missed by other scavengers he didn't know, but he took them gratefully. That afternoon he and Sampson used two of the sticks to support one end of their piece of canvas. It gave them a little patch of shade against the hot sun. And that night, when a thundershower came, it shed most of the rain. Ben had had the forethought to place their tin can where it would catch the runoff, and for once they had water that didn't have to be carried from the river.

Next morning a new batch of prisoners arrived. Ben watched the reception given them from a quarter of a mile away and saw the Spoilers move in to snatch everything of value. It made him angry, but there was nothing he and Rocky could do against twenty or thirty armed thugs.

"Some day," said the stonecutter, "I'd like to git a bunch o' decent boys together an' go after 'em. If we could take 'em by surprise, we might beat 'em so bad they'd give up stealin'."

Ben found that hard to believe. "McKenna's gang?" he said. "I reckon you'd have to kill 'em first."

"Well," Rocky replied mildly, "mebbe that's what I had in mind."

*　　*　　*

The prisoner population when they came to Belle Isle was about two thousand, and it didn't seem to vary much as the days passed. Not many new captives were being brought in, while at least an equal number died or were taken off to the hospital.

Sampson was in low spirits. His thick body needed a lot more nourishment than the scanty rations he received, and he seemed to lose interest in things after a few days. Most of the time he sat and brooded under the canvas awning.

It was curiosity that kept Ben going. He explored every

inch of the island inside the deadline, studying the shore and the current of the river. Also he watched the movements of the sentries. Each one walked a regular beat of about a hundred yards, met the next guard, then turned and slouched back. It took a lot of men to patrol the whole island, but now that there was a lull in the fighting, there seemed to be plenty of soldiers in Richmond. The guard, Ben figured, was changed every six hours.

As for the prisoners themselves, he had learned to know quite a few of them by sight. Those who had been there longest showed the fact in their looks. Their faces were blackened by sunburn and grime, their garments a mass of filthy rags held together with bits of string.

There was practically no way for a man to wash himself or his clothes at Belle Isle. So they went unbelievably dirty, their long, stringy hair and beards crawling with vermin. Yet it wasn't disgust but sympathy that Ben felt for them. In spite of their misery, a few individuals kept sunny and cheerful. In the evenings they would get together and sing, in cracked, hoarse voices. Their favorite tunes were hymns, learned in childhood, but there were also sad songs like "Tenting Tonight" and "Jeanie with the Light Brown Hair."

Ben learned the simple life histories of a number of men, for they were desperately homesick and liked to talk about familiar scenes and events back in New Hampshire, or Indiana, or Michigan. One of the prisoners he knew best was Sam Nelson, the young man from the Ninth Wisconsin.

"I used to help Dad in the gristmill," he told Ben. "Our place was on Rock River, in Jefferson County. There was woods all round, an' lakes full o' fish. My sisters used to pick blueberries for Ma to make into pies, but me—I liked to fish. Golly, how good a mess o' bluegills'd taste right now!"

Much of their conversation was naturally about food.

When they compared notes, Ben found Maine and Wisconsin cookery seemed to be a lot alike. And the lakes and streams and forests sounded like his home state, too.

"Think you'll ever get back there, Sam?" he asked the Wisconsin soldier.

Sam Nelson shook his head. "I hate to think about that," he said soberly. "Course, I won't give up hopin', but I ain't at all sure I'll live another winter if the war keeps on."

"Maybe you won't have to stay here." Ben tried to encourage him. "I've heard tell some prisoners get exchanged. Or you might be shipped off to another prison. You don't reckon any place could be worse'n Belle Isle, do you?"

"I dunno," said Sam. "I heard a feller yesterday talkin' about a prison down in Georgia. He was just brought in an' he'd heard a rumor about this place—Andersonville or some such name. Said it was run by Rebels that wanted to kill as many Yankees as the Rebs that died at Gettysburg. I reckon Belle Isle ain't quite that bad."

11

Escape

Ben had been on the island a little over a week. He had learned the prison routine and knew how to keep out of trouble. In spite of the poor food and the lack of shelter, he kept reasonably well, and his leg wound had healed to the point where it no longer hurt him. He exercised regularly, kept as clean as he could, and refused to give up hope. It was the men who didn't care any more who grew weak and sick.

One morning Sam Nelson didn't show up for rations. He was still missing at roll call, and Ben hurried to the place where his friend usually slept to see what was the matter. In spite of the broiling sun overhead, he found Sam huddled under his blanket, shaking with a chill. When he felt the young man's forehead, it was very hot and his eyes were feverishly bright.

"G-got the shakes," Sam said through chattering teeth. "It's the f-fever an' aiger."

A corporal and a guard approached about that time, looking for men who had failed to answer the roll, and Ben showed them the sick prisoner.

"Sho' is shakin', ain't he?" one of the Confederates remarked. "You better git him to the surgeon. Come on—step lively an' tote him down to the gate."

110

Nelson wasn't heavy. He was smaller-boned than Ben, and his long stay at Belle Isle had wasted away his muscles. Without too much trouble, the Maine boy lifted him, blanket and all, and carried him down the hill. At the gate a guard relieved him of his burden. The last Ben saw of his friend he was being lugged into the dingy building that served as a hospital.

For three days Ben waited hopefully for Sam to reappear, but it was useless. After that he knew that he must get away from Belle Isle, and soon. A desperate plan had been forming in his mind, and at last he told Joe Sampson about it.

"Look, Rocky," he said. "Look at all these men around us. Half of 'em are sick—even dyin'. An' the longer they stay here, the less they care what happens to 'em. We've got to get out, Joe, 'fore we find ourselves in the same fix. I've figgered a way, too, if you'll listen."

The big man shrugged. "Ain't got a chance," he said. "There's no boats on the island an' nothin' to build one out of. So what do you plan to do—sneak past all them guards an' hide on the ferry?"

"No, Joe. I've got a better plan than that. You know that low, swampy ground beyond the latrines, at the east end of the island? I've watched the sentries down that way. I bet we could get past 'em and crawl right through the reeds, clear down to the shore. All we need's a dark, wet night. Then we could swim across the river to the end o' the railroad bridge, just above the falls. I know the current runs fast, but I'm willin' to try it if you are."

Sampson's grin had a funny look. "Only trouble with that," he said, "is that I can't swim a stroke. But you go ahead, Ben. I'll take my chances stayin' alive till I'm exchanged or Richmond's captured."

The news that his husky friend didn't know how to swim

left Ben thunderstruck. It had never occurred to him that his attempt to escape would separate them, and at first he decided to give it up. Then came a rumor on the prison grapevine that made him change his mind. First he heard that there was heavy fighting down around Petersburg and a lot of fresh prisoners would be coming in. Soon after that he learned that many of the men now on the island were about to be shipped south by rail—to Andersonville, so the story went.

From what he had heard about the place, Ben thought he would rather die than be sent there. And with Sampson's help and encouragement, he got ready to make his try for freedom.

For days, now, he had felt himself growing gradually weaker. If he hoped to succeed, he knew he must have all his strength, and for that he needed real food.

"Rocky," he told his companion, "you know more about tradin' with the guards than I do. Maybe you could swap my sewin' kit for some meat an' bread. I'll give you that dollar I've still got, too, so you can get some for yourself."

Sampson insisted that Ben should hang on to the dollar, but he did consent to take the little canvas "housewife." Out of it Ben kept a spool of coarse white thread and a paper of pins, leaving the scissors, needles, and the rest of the thread in their case. That afternoon Joe went over toward the gate and managed to attract a guard's attention. It took a deal of dickering to get what he wanted, but before dark he returned with a parcel wrapped in newspaper.

"Here you be, son," he said. " 'Tain't as much as I'd wish, but it ought to put a mite o' muscle back on you."

The package contained three onions, half a dozen potatoes, a piece of tough, stringy meat that Ben suspected was mule, half a loaf of stale white bread, and a little salt.

"All the makin's of a stew," said Rocky. "You go forage for some firewood, an' I'll start gittin' it ready."

They ate their fill that night, and regardless of what the meat might be, Ben thought no meal had ever tasted quite so good. There were even a couple of potatoes and a little bread left over. He wrapped these carefully in a bit of oilcloth he had found in a deserted shebang and tied them inside his waistband. Before he went to sleep, he used his knife to rip the stripes from the sides of his trouser legs and stuffed the tapes in his pocket. Northern uniform pants were common enough among the Rebels, but he wanted to be as inconspicuous as possible. Now all he needed was a change in the weather, and it came sooner than he expected.

The air had been sultry, with occasional brief thundershowers. Now, on the day after his feast of stew, the skies were overcast and a steady drizzle began. As the evening grew darker, he finished his preparations and said good-by to Sampson.

"If you hear shootin'," he said, "you'll know they probably got me. But I couldn't stand it not to try."

"Shucks, boy—you'll make it," the big fellow assured him. "And," he added wistfully, "give my regards to Ike Bean an' Morrison an' the rest o' the Twentieth Maine."

*   *   *

There was a mist hanging over the river when Ben stole down the slope. If he had ordered the weather personally, it could hardly have been better for his plan. The sentries, he knew, would find nothing unusual in a prisoner's visiting the latrines at that hour. There was so much dysentery that men had to make the trip night and day.

When he reached the trenches, it was so dark that he doubted if the sentries had even seen him. He could hear their voices and the slow shuffle of their footsteps beyond the deadline, but they were invisible through the mist.

For a little while he crouched there in the foul-smelling dark. Luckily no other prisoners were near at the moment, and he had a chance to get his bearings. Crawling on his stomach, he reached the drainage ditch that ran down to the riverbank. From watching the guards he knew that two of them ended their beats on either side of the ditch and that they would hail each other when they met.

The ditch was perhaps a hundred yards long, and the sentries would be about halfway down its length. He eased himself into the slime and inched along, almost nauseated by the filth around him.

It was impossible to tell how much distance he had made, but after a time he heard voices quite distinctly, coming from not more than twenty feet away.

"Ever'thin' quiet, Bill?" one guard asked.

"Yeah, they're behavin' theirselves—tryin' to keep dry, I reckon. Sho' is a lousy night, though, ain't it?"

"Mis'able. Makes this ditch stink worse'n ever. Be glad when they put me on another part o' the line."

"Well, so long, now."

And two sets of footsteps moved slowly off into the rain and the dark.

Ben began crawling again. As the sounds faded to silence, he went as fast as he could, still on his hands and knees. Soon he could catch a new sound, the swish of the river as it ran past the end of the ditch. Looking up, he saw that he had reached the cover of the reeds along the shore. Should he try it now or wait for the sentries to meet and separate again?

With a shiver of impatience he made his decision. The guards, he thought, were probably at the opposite ends of their beats by now. But more than that he had an intense desire to wash the nastiness off his clothes and his hands. So, creeping another dozen feet to the river's edge and drawing a long breath, he pushed off silently into the current.

It was a great deal swifter and more powerful than he had thought. In a moment of panic he struck out vigorously with his arms and made a considerable splash.

"Hey!" he heard a sentry call. "You hear that, Bill?"

Within seconds there came the bang of a musket and a bullet cut the water a few feet from Ben's head. He gasped a lungful of air and dove like a muskrat. The shot had put real fear into him, and he swam underwater for what seemed a long way. When he dared to lift his head again, he could see a dim flicker of light on the farther bank, where he knew the railroad trestle must be. It was off to his right. Either he had misjudged his direction or the current was carrying him too fast. Desperately he turned, swimming upstream from the light.

There was another rifle shot about then, but it came nowhere near him. And a moment later he heard the sentry's voice again.

"Don't seem to be nothin' out there," he was calling to his neighbor. "Must ha' been a fish jumped."

The words brought Ben only partial relief, for he still had an awful dread of being carried over the falls. He swam frantically, angling to the right, across the pull of the river. Little by little he seemed to be gaining, but the effort was taking a lot out of him. The distance he had to cover was nearly half a mile in a straight line, but because of the current, he would have to swim twice that far, and already he was very tired.

It was the fear of death and sheer, dogged desperation that took him the last hundred yards. He crawled feebly out on the stones at the foot of the bridge abutment and collapsed, gasping for breath. How long he lay there, half in the water, he never knew, but it must have been twenty minutes or more. At last he pulled himself up out of the river and sat looking off into the mist. The falls made a deep, rumbling roar, but on Belle Isle everything seemed to be quiet. The alarm caused by the shooting had subsided, and he was pretty certain that his absence wouldn't be noticed until the noon roll call. What time had it been when he started? There was no sure way to tell, but he thought it must have been about ten o'clock. If so, it was getting close to midnight, but he would have five or six hours of darkness to get clear of the city.

Ben dragged himself to his feet, still dripping wet, and started cautiously eastward along the riverbank. Beyond the railroad bridge, there was an area of small warehouses and empty lots. And the bank, along the side of the falls, was built up with stone to keep it from washing away. Ben had to make his way on the top of this embankment, but he went carefully, watching at the mouth of every alley or vacant lot to make sure nobody was there to see him pass. Very few people were likely to be out on such a night, but he could take no chances.

A mile or more below the place where he had crawled ashore, he went under the second railroad trestle. A train of freight cars was puffing its way across, and he stayed in the shadows till the engine headlight was well past. Mayo's Bridge—the main wagon bridge to Manchester and the south —loomed ahead of him in the rainy dark. Still keeping close to the bank, he crept under the huge timber supports and moved on without being seen.

He was now three or four miles below Belle Isle, but across the river the dim street lights showed there was a lot of the city yet to be passed. So far, he congratulated himself, he had done pretty well. But there was one hazard it might be harder to avoid. That was a possible chance meeting with some of Winder's detectives.

General Winder, he had heard, was in charge of all military prisons in the South, and his headquarters were here in Richmond. He had gathered a formidable group of men to hunt down spies and escaping Yankees—men with noses like bloodhounds, so the rumor went. At the thought Ben grinned. He would have been easy to smell out if he hadn't made that long swim across the river. As it was, he was probably cleaner right now than he had been in a month.

Ben had no way of knowing whether Winder's sleuths prowled the Manchester side of the James, but it seemed likely. His hair and his ragged clothes were still dripping. If he were seen now, would that fact betray him? It had poured hard earlier in the night, but now the drizzle had eased off, and he doubted if merely walking in the rain would have made anybody as wet as he was. So it behooved him to go even more carefully until he had dried out.

A moment later he was startled to hear footsteps in the alley just ahead. Somebody was coming slowly over the cobbles toward the river. Ben pulled back around the corner and cowered there against the brick wall of an old factory building. After a few heartbeats the man appeared. He made no effort to move quietly, and his boots clumped heavily on the stones. Then, to Ben's relief, the stranger scrambled down the bank to the water's edge. Looking down, he could see there was a small skiff tied there, and the man got into it, rattling a pair of oars as he stepped aft.

Ben expected to see him untie the boat. Instead, he fumbled for something under the stern thwart, picked it up with a grunt of pleasure, and came ponderously climbing back up the embankment. It was too dark to see what he had recov-

ered, but from the gurgling sounds he heard, Ben was fairly sure it was a bottle of liquor. He waited there, shivering, until the footfalls went off up the alley and gradually became too faint to hear.

Then as quietly as possible, he climbed down the embankment for a closer look at the boat. There was no chain or padlock. The bow was simply tied by a rope to a ring set in the rocks, and at the discovery Ben's heart hammered faster. Perhaps he had better revise his whole plan of escape.

12

The James

For several minutes he crouched there by the skiff, weighing the advantages and disadvantages of using it. He would be a lot more conspicuous in a boat on the river, but he could move faster. If he could get far enough below the city before daylight, his chances might be better than if he tried to make it on foot. Also, he intended to go down the left bank, and if he continued walking, it meant he would have to swim across the river once more.

Right or wrong, he decided that the boat gave him an opportunity he couldn't afford to pass up. Without further hesitation he untied the painter, climbed aboard, and pushed off.

When he put the oars in the rowlocks, they made a creaking noise, much louder than he liked. There seemed to be no way to row quietly, and for a moment panic seized him. Then he remembered the stripes he had cut off his trousers the previous morning. While the skiff drifted, he pulled the rumpled tapes out of his pocket and wound them quickly around both oars. Then he tried them in the locks. To his delight the squeaks and rattles were gone, and pulling on the oars, he slipped downstream as quietly as a shadow.

He had not gone very far when he heard a clink of metal

somewhere ahead. He rested on his oars and turned to look, and there, not a hundred yards away, was a huge, dark mass on the water. It was a Confederate gunboat, moored in the middle of the river. The sound he had heard must be an anchor chain grating against the hawsehole.

Ben swung his body around on the thwart, facing forward. From now on he resolved to row in that position so that he could see what lay ahead. Soundlessly he propelled the skiff to the left, away from the gunboat, and drifted past, holding his breath as he listened for sounds aboard her. Luckily the men on watch must have been looking the other way, for there was no hail from the deck. He waited till the shape of the ship was lost in the darkness astern before he started rowing again.

Far off to the left, on top of a hill in the city, Ben heard a church bell strike three times. It meant that daybreak would come in less than two more hours, and he had better be ashore by then. Swinging the bow of the boat to the left, he approached the farther bank and studied the outlines of such buildings as could be seen. The factories and warehouses had been left behind. All he could make out now was an occasional shanty down at the water's edge.

He was slipping along within twenty yards of the shore when another gunboat loomed up on his right, and this time he heard some voices coming from the larger craft.

"Think the Yankees'll try it by the river?" one man asked.

"Shucks!" Another voice chuckled. "Wish they would! Them big batteries on Drewry's Bluff'd blow 'em clean out o' water. Besides, there's the barriers we helped set, an' all them torpedoes in the channel. Ain't a chance if you ask me."

The voices faded in the distance, and Ben rested on his oars, thinking. "Torpedoes" had an ugly sound. He knew they were explosive mines floating in the water, ready to blow up if a boat struck them. The thought shook him a little.

Since he had no idea where the torpedoes were located, he decided he would rather take his chances on solid ground. For another twenty minutes he rowed slowly in the shadow of the bank. There were fewer houses now. For long stretches he saw only open fields and bushes, and he thought it would be safe to put ashore. Nosing the boat in on the mud, he climbed out, removed the tapes from the oars, gave the craft a shove, and watched it drift away down the river.

Ben stuck his head above the bank and looked around. Now that the rain had stopped, he could see better, and there seemed to be no house or sign of life anywhere near. He crawled up under the shelter of a clump of brush and went to sleep, for the night's labors had brought him to the point of complete exhaustion.

Just at sunup he was wakened by the barking of a dog. The sound startled him—made him think of bloodhounds. Perhaps his flight from the island had been noticed and the alarm was already out. Fearfully he peered out from his hiding place and saw a small farm dog dashing along on the trail of a rabbit. Ben grinned. The sight was reassuring, and at the same time it reminded him that he, too, was hungry.

The piece of bread he took from the oilcloth bag at his waist was somewhat soggy, but he ate it with a ravenous appetite. Where was his next meal coming from? He didn't know, but it was high time he did something about it. The field behind him was planted to some kind of vegetables, he could see. He stole out cautiously and pulled up a couple of the tops. To his delight two respectable-sized carrots came out of the ground—the first such food he had seen in months. He gnawed on them like a squirrel and reveled in the taste.

Back in the brush clump once more, Ben cut a long,

straight shoot that would do for a fish pole. With the strong cotton thread for a line and a bent pin for a hook, he had something that at least resembled fishing tackle. He put it over his shoulder and sauntered boldly on down the shore.

When he came to a place that looked as if there might be fish in the water, he dug a few worms for bait and sat down on the bank to try his luck. A pebble tied into the line served as a sinker. If any fish were around, he was sure the wriggling worm would attract them.

Just about that time he heard the chunking of paddles and saw a Rebel gunboat come nosing slowly down the river. It was near enough for some of the men on deck to wave at him, so he waved back.

"Hi!" one of them called. "Gettin' any fish?"

"Hain't cotched nothin' yit," Ben replied in his broadest Southern accent. And the sailors laughed and waved again as the craft steamed on.

The sun warmed him and dried the last moisture out of his ragged clothes. He began to have more confidence now. Certainly his disguise—a shiftless countryman out fishing— was about as good as he could have found.

Ten minutes later, to his surprise, he felt a nibble at the end of his line. He raised the pole a little, felt the fish still on the hook, and lifted quickly, throwing his catch out on the bank. It was unfamiliar to him but must be some kind of good-sized sunfish, eight or nine inches long. He knew it would taste wonderful if he could fry it in a skillet with fat pork.

Since he had no fire, no frying pan, and no fat, there was only one thing to do. He trimmed off the head and tail, gutted and scaled the fish with his knife, and devoured it raw. Strangely enough it didn't taste bad. He began to feel some strength coming back into his thin body.

It was time now to resume his journey. First he pulled two or three more carrots to take along in his pocket. Then, with the pole over his shoulder and a cheerful whistle on his lips, he set off along the bank. After the rain the air was cooler. It was a fine morning for traveling.

Ben's idea of the geography of that part of Virginia was rather vague. He knew the James flowed south below Richmond and then swung eastward again, more or less parallel with the Chickahominy. Where the Union Army might be, he wasn't sure. But if it was true that they were attacking Petersburg, they must have crossed the James somewhere within twenty miles of where he was now.

There was a road a quarter of a mile or so off to his left. He kept one eye on it as he hiked southward, and soon he saw a cloud of dust approaching from the direction of Richmond. A troop of Confederate cavalry went by at an easy canter, paying no attention to the lone figure by the river. Next he saw the familiar signs of earthworks, built at right angles to the road and across it. Several companies of Rebel infantry lolled there in the trenches, and the smoke of their breakfast fires drifted down to him. This, he figured, must be one of their lines of defense—he hoped the last one.

The infantry, as might have been expected, had pickets out. One of them, down near the river, started to challenge Ben but thought better of it.

"Hi," he said with a grin. "How's fishin'?"

"On'y cotched one," Ben replied. "Not a very big 'un, either."

"So? Where is he?"

"I et him." Ben chuckled. "But they's still some in the river. Why don't ye try it?"

"Hah!" said the sentry. "Ain't much of a chance o' that. We're busy lookin' fer Yanks."

If Ben shivered at those words, he didn't show it. With the pole still on his shoulder, he went on his way. The road curved off to the left, but he stayed near the bank, as anyone going fishing would have done. As he went along, he saw occasional gunboats cruising up and down the channel, and a little farther down there was a long barrier of chains and piling, extending clear across the river. This must be what the men on the Confederate warship had been talking about when he heard them in the night.

Ahead of him he saw a white-painted fence, with green, sloping lawns beyond. Up to the left in a grove of tall trees was a fine, big mansion. The lawn extended all the way to the water, and Ben had no choice but to climb the fence and go boldly on. He crossed a graveled walk, leading down to the riverbank. At its foot was a pier where several boats were moored. In ordinary times, he supposed, the rich people who lived here must use the river as a highway up to the city.

Before he had gone many steps farther, a man in riding boots came striding toward him from the direction of the house. He had a long-lashed whip under his arm, and he scowled as he drew near. No doubt he was the overseer of the plantation—a harsh and cruel man, if what Ben had read in *Uncle Tom's Cabin* was true. Ben concealed his shaking and put on the most half-witted expression he could manage.

"What you doin' here?" the overseer demanded. "Don't you know this is private property?"

"Y-yassuh," Ben stammered. "Ah'm on'y g-goin' down the river to fish. My maw's sick an' got to have somethin' to eat."

"Where you come from?"

"Long ways up yon'—mos' to Richmon'."

"Well—get on with you, then. But when you come back, don't cross these lawns. Go up around by the road."

Ben nodded. "Ah won' come back this way, suh," he mumbled quite truthfully. Then he hurried on, still feeling the man's suspicious stare in the back of his neck. He reached the fence on the south side of the plantation, clambered over, and heaved a sigh of relief. He had had some close calls, and this was one of the closest.

He didn't stop till he had put more than a mile between himself and the plantation house. On his left was a field where a few Negroes were at work. The crop looked like tobacco. What he wanted was more vegetables, so he kept on, looking occasionally at the sun to judge the time and the direction.

It was now well along in the forenoon, but Ben knew he still had a considerable distance to travel. About midday he skirted another field where some kind of root crop was growing. A careful look up and down the river showed no one in sight, and he pulled up one of the plants. When he shook off the dirt, he was pleased to find two or three small yams attached to the stalk. They wouldn't be fit to eat raw, but he took them along anyway, hopeful that sooner or later he could build a fire.

As it turned out, that time arrived much more quickly than he expected. He saw a curl of smoke rising from a deserted bivouac, a short distance up from the bank. A Confederate picket squad must have stopped there to cook a noon meal. There were signs of half a dozen fires, but only one still showed hot embers. Hastily Ben gathered more dry sticks and soon had a flame going. Then he thrust the little sweet potatoes into the coals and went down to the bank to do some more fishing while they roasted.

Once more his luck was good. Within half an hour he had a fat sunfish to add to his dinner, and this time he cooked it over the fire, along with a pinch of salt. By the time the yams were done, he was ready to enjoy what seemed to him a luxurious meal.

As soon as it was eaten, he hurried on again, for he knew his fisherman's disguise would not do for traveling at night. What he had to do was make as many miles as possible in daylight. His best estimate was that he had now come at least ten miles from Richmond.

Over across the river, he could see a glint of sun on metal. It was a long way off, but he was able to make out the lines of ramparts, high on a bluff, and the muzzles of many cannon in the emplacements. This must be the fort—Drewry's Bluff —that the sailors had mentioned. It certainly commanded the approach by water and would make things hot for any Yankee fleet that tried to come up the river.

That afternoon Ben passed several more plantations, but he was careful to go around by the road. Whenever he met a vehicle or people on foot, he shambled along, scuffing his bare feet in the dust, and tried to look as stupid as possible. One lady in a fine carriage sniffed as she went past and remarked to her companion that these poor whites were "disgusting."

Between such encounters he stepped up his pace. The woods, back from the river, were tempting, but he thought it likely that Rebel patrols would be using them for cover. He saw none of the landmarks he had noticed weeks earlier when he was being marched to prison. That route, he was sure, had been much farther from the James.

It was about five o'clock when he cut across the neck of an oxbow in the river. After that the road along the bank swung east again, then northeast to another big bend. He was some distance beyond this point when darkness began to fall. Ahead of him was a hill with woods on it that looked as if they might give him concealment. But as he approached, he saw that many of the trees were shattered and splintered. He had seen enough battlefields to know this was one. Artillery had been used here, and soon he came on broken wheels, rusty guns, and the bleached skeletons of horses lying there in the desolation. Long afterward he learned that he had stumbled on the scene of the battle of Malvern Hill, fought two years before.

It wasn't a comfortable place to sleep. He turned back to the right and found himself a nest in a thicket of jack pine near the road.

13

Petersburg

One of the first things Ben saw when he woke next morning was a deep trench and earthworks less than a hundred feet away. Frightened, he ducked back into the pine thicket and took a cautious look around. The dirt seemed to be fairly fresh. It looked as if it had been dug only a few days before, but the soldiers who had manned the entrenchment were nowhere to be seen.

Reassured by the complete silence of the early morning, he crept out once more and examined the fortified position. Since it faced eastward, he was sure it was the work of the Confederate Army, probably prepared when Grant was expected to attack up the river. Now it had been abandoned.

Ben still had a bite or two of bread, and he ate it for breakfast along with a raw carrot. Then he went back to the road and continued eastward. Off to his right he could see the James through the trees. He seemed to be near the head of another big bend, for below the place where he stood the river swung sharply to the south.

He looked again and rubbed his eyes. It was more than a mile to the farther bank, but he could have sworn he saw patches of blue moving over there. After a moment his curiosity got the better of his judgment, and he left the road, cutting across the fields toward the riverbank.

Suddenly, without any warning, three Rebel soldiers rose out of the grass to bar his way.

"Whar you think yo' goin'?" a grating voice asked him.

Ben hoped he looked as foolish as he felt. "Ah jes' figgered to ketch me some fish," he mumbled. "Is them Yankees over yon'?"

"Sho' is. We got ol' Ben Butler's army bottled up in the bend o' the river. Yo' lookin' at what they call Bermuda Hundred, an' we're yeah to keep watch on it. So, you better make tracks out'n this, 'fore somebody fills you full o' lead."

Ben didn't stay to argue. He grinned sheepishly, shouldered his fish pole, and went back to the road. After a mile or two, he came to a fork. The road to the right headed southward, paralleling the river but a good distance from it. There was no signpost to show where it led, but a marker on the main road pointed east and read "Charles City Court House, 10 mi." He decided to take the southerly fork.

The road showed signs of having been well traveled at one time, but now it must be little used. Grass had sprung up between the old wheel ruts, and for several miles he encountered nobody moving in either direction. Then, a long way ahead, he saw horses coming at a gallop. There was a ditch close at hand, and he tumbled into it, pulling the tall weeds together to screen him. After a few moments the beat of hoofs grew louder. A detachment of Confederate cavalry spurred past, the horses flecked with lather.

Ben waited to make sure no more of them were coming, and when the coast was clear, he scrambled out again and resumed his journey. It was certain nobody would have recognized his blue uniform pants now. The dust of the roads had coated them a yellowish dun color that might have passed for a Rebel's butternut gray. It had stained his old shirt, too, and was matted into his hair. He could even taste the grit of it in his mouth.

After the cavalry had ridden out of sight, the countryside went back to its lonesome stillness. Footsore and weary as he was, Ben's spirits were high. He was really free! No matter what new dangers might come his way, he had the confident feeling he could cope with them.

The road climbed over a little rise, and there, abruptly, he found the river right in front of him. It had broadened out amazingly to a width of what looked like three or four miles. But the thing that thrilled him most was the sight of gunboats anchored on the near shore—Union gunboats—flying the Stars and Stripes!

He forgot all about being tired. At full speed, under the noonday sun, he raced down the long slope, vaulting fences, and plowing through brush. When he reached the bank, he was panting hard and stopped a moment to catch his breath. Half a mile down the shore, he could see a long pier built of new yellow lumber. There was a steamboat tied up there, taking on cargo. And above, on the bank, were a lot of men in blue uniforms.

Ben started walking in that direction. Through force of habit, he still carried his pole, and he didn't realize he had it until a Union sentry stepped out from behind a tree and pointed a rifle at him.

"Halt!" he commanded. "No civilians are allowed 'round here."

"L-look," Ben stammered. "I'm no civilian. I got away from Belle Isle Prison night 'fore last. I'm a Yankee private from the Twentieth Maine."

"That story don't go down with me," the sentry told him scornfully. "You Rebs are tricky when it comes to spyin'. Git, now, 'fore I let daylight into you!"

Ben was desperate. "Wait," he pleaded. "I'm tellin' you the truth. Joe Sampson an' I were captured more'n three weeks back. Both of us are from Company B, Twentieth Maine Volunteers. Cap'n Morrill or Sergeant Gray—they'd vouch for me."

The soldier's suspicions were beginning to weaken. "You got anything on you to prove it?" he asked.

Ben thought fast. "Only one thing," he said, and pulled a damp, bedraggled little Bible from the depths of his pocket. "I had to swim about a mile, so this got pretty wet. But mebbe you can still read what it says here in the front."

The writing on the flyleaf was blurred and indistinct, but Ben was able to point out some of the words.

"Here at the top," he said, "is where my ma wrote. It says 'To my son Benjamin, Christmas, 1863.' An' you can read the next line better. Look an' see for yourself."

The sentry spelled it out slowly. "Private Ben Everett," he read. "20th Me. Vol. Rgt."

"Well," said Ben, "you believe me now, don't you?"

"Yeah, I reckon so. Hey, Dan! Pass this man on down the line. Claims he's a Yankee prisoner escaped from Belle Isle, an' he's lookin' for his regiment. Watch him close, though. Might be a trick."

Ben moved on from one sentry to the next. Some of them were curious to know how he had managed to get off the prison island. Others professed to doubt his story until he showed them the Bible. But at last he arrived at the busy area by the pier. It was noon then, and the steamer was just about loaded, so some of the work units were knocking off for dinner. A quartermaster sergeant listened to Ben's account of his adventures and decided he could take a chance on sending him across the river.

"They'll know better what to do with ye over to City P'int," he said.

"Thanks," Ben replied feelingly. "I've been travelin' quite a ways, an' I'm hungry. You got a piece o' hardtack to spare?"

The sergeant did better than that. Like most men in the Quartermaster Corps, he ate well, and he gave Ben a smoking plate of meat with beans and white bread. Then the steamer's whistle blew, and Ben was hustled aboard. He stood near the bow, watching the busy traffic of transports and gunboats in the river, conscious that every thrust of the paddles took him nearer to his friends at the front.

When they docked at City Point, he had to answer questions all over again. It seemed a lot of civilians posing as stray Union soldiers had been caught spying, so the interrogation was thorough. It was late in the afternoon when the captain who had quizzed him finally wrote out a paper that would get him through the lines.

"Young man," he said, "you've given us more information about Belle Isle and the conditions there than we've been able to get before. You had quite an experience. I hope you'll be as lucky through the rest of the war."

Ben was soon fitted out with a brand-new uniform, knapsack, and blanket, as well as a used but serviceable rifle. Once more he felt like a real soldier. He started toward Petersburg that evening, slept in the woods a few miles east of the city, and pushed on again at daybreak.

That was the tenth of July. Nearly a month had gone by since Ben's capture, and to him it seemed like half a lifetime. It took him most of the day to locate the Third Brigade, and when he did so, he entered a totally strange world. The siege trenches in front of Petersburg were like nothing he had ever seen before or even imagined. They made him think of a vast,

sprawling network of woodchuck holes. When he finally
found the Twentieth Maine, it was in a section of earthworks
fairly close to the Confederate lines. The trenches were deeper
than a tall man's head and were connected in all directions
with communication trenches and bombproof shelters. These
bombproofs were something new in Ben's experience. They
were roofed with logs and earth—hot, airless cellars under
the ground. He couldn't figure why they were needed at first.
Then he heard the whistle of a mortar shell and saw the pro-

jectile drop straight down into a trench fifty feet away, blowing dirt, rocks, and bits of logs high into the air when it exploded.

By that time he had reported to his captain and been greeted by dozens of friends.

"Them mortar bombs," big Ed Morrison explained, "are an invention o' the devil. When you hear one a-comin', duck. There's only one thing worse in this kind o' fightin', an' that's a Rebel sharpshooter. We had an awful lot o' snipin' back an' forth when we first dug in. Now, though, we sort o' stick to the rules an' leave each other be."

Not all of Ben's old acquaintances were still there. Several had been killed or wounded when the Army made its first all-out attacks against the Confederate trenches. And after they had settled down to siege warfare, one Company B man was shot by a Rebel sniper. He was from Wiscasset, a young fellow hardly older than Ben. One morning he woke up, yawned, and staggered to his feet in a front-line trench. The next instant a bullet went through his head.

Ben also grieved for his prison companion, Rocky Joe Sampson. It had been hard to leave him on Belle Isle, and what might happen to him now was a painful question. If only the Federals could take Petersburg, Richmond would be almost sure to fall. Sometimes Ben prayed that he might be in the first wave of attackers, so that he could help liberate the prisoners.

In some ways the inactive life in the trenches was almost as miserable as fighting in the Wilderness had been. The weather was unusually hot, even for July. There had been little rain, and the red dust rose in choking clouds, getting into the men's eyes and mouths, spoiling the food they tried to eat. Water was scarce, too, and none could be spared for bathing or washing clothes. Such luxuries were enjoyed only by regiments relieved from front-line duty.

The Twentieth Maine was ordered to move a few days after Ben rejoined the outfit, and he found himself in a part of the line somewhat farther from the Rebel trenches. They were still in plain sight, but a clump of trees stood in the no man's land between the lines, giving them occasional shade.

Since there was now a sort of gentlemen's agreement against sniper fire, several of the Maine men, with others from Michigan and Massachusetts regiments, sat under the trees one day to play cards. The game hadn't been going long when a grass fire started, a few yards away. One of the Yankees ran to stamp it out, and a Confederate sentry lost his head. His bullet broke the Union man's arm. The card players pulled him back and ran for cover, while the whole Third Brigade yelled epithets at the faithless enemy.

It turned out that the Rebels were just as upset by the incident as they were. The following morning the man who had fired the shot was forced to walk back and forth on the top of the parapet with a log tied to his shoulders. The Confederates called out, inviting the Yankees to shoot him, but nobody did so. Seeing him properly punished was all the satisfaction they wanted.

There were always rumors flying up and down the curving ten-mile line in front of Petersburg. Most of them didn't amount to much, but there was one that persisted day after day in that hot July. As Ben heard it, the story went that a regiment of Pennsylvania coal miners in Burnside's corps were digging a tunnel all the way under the middle of the Rebel entrenchments. When it was finished, an enormous quantity of gunpowder was to be exploded. "And," said the New Hampshire soldier who told him about it, "if I was you, I'd git wads o' cotton to stick in your ears. She's goin' to be a real humdinger!"

Many of the men pooh-poohed the idea, yet even the scoffers showed a certain amount of nervousness. At last the word was passed that the date of the big blast had been set. Then came definite orders to the Twentieth Maine and other regiments of the Fifth Corps. They were to get ready for action the evening of July 29.

14

The Crater

The Maine soldiers were in a section of the trenches some half a mile south of the Confederate fort where the huge mine was supposed to explode, but their location gave them a fine view of the fort, off to their right. The blast, they learned, was timed to go off at three-thirty in the morning. As soon as the Union forces were sure the line had been broken, a storming column from the Ninth Corps was to make an assault. After they had won a foothold, the Twentieth Maine was to open a heavy fire and then advance.

As the hour approached, every man in the regiment was on his feet, his head above the parapet for a better view. If the Rebels had known it, a lot of splendid targets were offered to snipers, but no shots came.

Then suddenly the ground shook under their feet, and there was a vast, muffled roar. The fort in the Southern lines went toward the sky in a mass of flame, smoke, and earth. Men, guns, timbers were all hurled high into the air.

Ben was shocked and numbed by the sight. It was the most terrible carnage he had ever witnessed. Hardly had the bodies stopped falling when the Union artillery opened up along the whole length of the line. The steady thunder was almost deafening. Then Ben saw the attackers from the Ninth Corps struggling to get out of their own trenches. Nothing had been done to clear a path for them, and they had to climb the parapets, break through tangles of spiked posts, cross the hundred yards between the lines, and charge the Confederate entrenchments. Among them were a division of colored troops, proud to have been chosen for the job.

Once clear of the entanglements, they charged up to the place where the fort had stood and came to a startled halt. Before them was a gigantic hole in the ground, a hundred and seventy feet long and thirty feet deep. But there was no time to stare at it, for other troops were crowding up from behind. Over the edge and into the crater they poured, many falling down the steep sides. And there they floundered, unable to climb out.

What had appeared as a wide-open gap in the Rebel lines turned out to be a terrible trap. Ben looked on in horror as Confederate guns, hastily turned on the crater, began slaughtering the helpless men who filled it.

There was no charge by the Fifth Corps because they had no place to go. General Warren, commanding the corps, went back and conferred with Meade. But it was obvious to all the Yankees in the front line by then that the great mine had gained them nothing. Some individual divisions were sent forward in gallant attacks that resulted only in more dead and wounded. Daylight came and with it a bitter musketry fire from the Rebel side. They were doubly angry—first because of the mine, but even more because the North had used Negro soldiers against them.

For the rest of that day and the two weeks that followed, the Maine men huddled in their trenches, stifled by the midsummer heat and the awful stench that came from the unburied corpses in the crater. The men of the regiment, Ben thought, were beginning to have a strange, wild look. They were thin as rails and burned black by the sun, and their red-rimmed eyes stared out of the caked dust like burnt holes in a blanket. If he had had a mirror, he would have seen he was no different from the rest.

Finally, on the night of August 14, the Fifth Corps was pulled out of the line and divisions of the Ninth Corps moved down to take over their area. Next morning the Twentieth Maine marched back to the wooded country in the rear with a chance to rest in peaceful surroundings.

Ben drew in long breaths of the sweet, pine-scented air. He rolled like a colt in the clean grass, beat the dust out of his clothes, and washed them in a small stream. Once more it was good to be alive.

Later that day the soldiers received the first mail they had had in a month. Ben got two letters. One of them had been written in June, before his mother had known that he was missing. It was a happy account of things at home and mentioned the good news about the war as reported in the Northern papers. Evidently the editors in Boston and Portland had a much rosier view of the fighting than the soldiers who were in it. Also enclosed was a short note from Ben's brother Abner, forgiving him and wishing him well.

The second letter made Ben want to cry. Mrs. Everett knew when she wrote it that he must have been killed or captured. The ink was blotted with her tears.

"You may never read this," she said. "But if in God's goodness you are spared to receive it, I want you to know you have been constantly in my prayers. Many times I have thought how little you had seen of life in your few years and how much you still had to live for. Yet I cannot find it in my heart to regret that you fought for what you knew was right. Now, wherever you may be, my love goes out to you."

Ben had written home briefly on the day he got back to

the regiment, but he knew the mails were slow. Now he sat down and wrote a full account of his being taken prisoner and his escape. "I guess, Mother," he said, "your prayers must have done some good. Anyhow, I was certainly taken care of, whether it was luck or a guardian angel. This war seems to drag awful slow, but I am confident we will win in the end. Then what fun it will be when I come home again!"

It wasn't obvious to the enlisted men, but the wheels of the North were still grinding. General Grant had a strategy that could hardly fail, given enough time. To begin with, Sherman's army in the West was steadily pushing Joe Johnston back toward Atlanta, and that city must soon fall. So Grant could concentrate on the formidable Army of Northern Virginia, still defending Richmond and Petersburg. Lee was outnumbered by the Union forces but couldn't be knocked out of his entrenchments. In one way or another he must be starved out.

Food for the Southern defenders came from two sources —the rich Shenandoah Valley and the equally fertile lowlands of the Carolinas and southern Virginia. Grant had plans to cut off both these supply routes. Phil Sheridan's army would take care of the Shenandoah. Eventually every field and pasture would be stripped clean, granaries burned, and the guerrilla bands stamped out in that area. As the grim commander-in-chief put it, "Even a crow traveling over the valley would have to carry his own provisions." And Lee would never again be able to use it as a highway to Maryland and Pennsylvania.

Petersburg was the key to the rail lines from the south, and once more Grant would try a flanking movement to the left, in an effort to cut them off.

So it came about that the Twentieth Maine didn't have long to rest. Early in the morning of August 18, they were issued three days' rations and lined up in marching order. A warm, steady rain had started to fall in the night.

"Wouldn't you know it?" Martin Preble grunted. "Reg'lar marchin' weather! But by gum I'd ruther be out in it than back in that stinkin' trench!"

They fell into column with the brigade, behind other units of the Fifth Corps. Deep mud made the artillery horses strain in their collars. Streams swollen by rain had to be waded. They left the pine woods behind and moved through open country, and by noon the corps was in sight of the Weldon Railroad.

There was only one trouble. The Confederates knew all about their expedition. During the morning there had been a skirmish with Rebel cavalry along their route, and although the gray riders had been driven off, General Lee must be pretty certain they were headed for the railroad. No sooner had they halted, near the Globe Tavern, than orders were given to dig in and wait for an attack.

The war-wise veterans of the Twentieth Maine didn't have to be told twice. They pitched in at once, cutting down trees and building breastworks. Then they settled down in the drizzle to wait.

Nothing happened that night, but the next morning they could hear heavy firing off to the north, where the Second and Third Divisions were dug in on a line crossing the railroad. The rain was coming down harder by then.

The Maine men, as part of the First Division, were holding the southern end of the line a few hundred yards west of the tracks. Once, after a rumor came that the fight was going badly north of them, the regiment was ordered out of its entrenchments and sent hurrying up the railroad to help the other divisions. But before long they were halted and marched back to their original position.

Beaten off in their first attack, the Confederate troops waited till the next morning, the twenty-first, to make their move against the Yankees' left flank. Actually they misjudged the location of the flank and came charging into a two-hundred-yard gap between Union divisions.

It was a sight Ben would never forget. The troops came out of the woods a quarter of a mile away, gray uniforms in solid attack formation, red flags fluttering above the green of the cornfield they had to cross. He felt almost sorry for them. This was like so many Yankee charges he had seen—naked courage against strong entrenchments. But the yelling Rebels didn't know they were in trouble yet. It must have appeared to them that they were about to roll up the Union flank.

To their complete confusion, they were suddenly under a fierce cross-fire from the south, where the Maine men lay behind their breastworks. Hundreds of the Confederates fell in the middle of their charge. Then other hundreds dropped their guns and came stumbling toward the Union trenches with hands in the air. It was one of the worst defeats the Rebels had suffered in years, and it cost the South the Weldon Railroad for the rest of the war.

As far as Ben's regiment went, it was the easiest victory they had ever had. Not a single man was killed or wounded! After the prisoners had been sent off to the rear, the Twentieth Maine settled down where they were to guard the railroad line. Once the rain stopped falling, it grew pleasant enough in that part of Virginia. The late August and September nights were fine for sleeping, and crops in the fields around them gave the foragers a chance to bring in better food. Ben and his companions lost some of their gaunt, worn-out look and put on a little weight.

This easy time lasted until late in the month of September. Much of the talk in the tents and around the campfires was about politics that fall. The Republicans had nominated Lincoln to run for president again in the November elections, while the Democratic party had made General McClellan their candidate. "Little Mac" had always been a hero to the men in the ranks. He was the perfect picture of a commander —well-groomed, splendidly mounted, dashing, and brave. More than that, they believed he took care of his soldiers.

Nominating McClellan looked like a master stroke for the Democrats. The enlisted men in the Northern armies made up a big share of the voters, and it was thought he would carry their ballots. But in the Twentieth Maine and many other veteran regiments the feeling didn't run that way.

The reason was that a main plank in the Democrats' platform had pronounced the war a failure and called for a stop to the fighting—a negotiated peace that would recognize the Confederate States and dissolve the Union.

"Mebbe we've lost a lot o' battles," Ike Bean said, putting his feeling into words. "Mebbe the war's cost too many lives. But, dadburn it, we ain't losin' now! What's been the good of all the hard marches an' fights we been through if we give up an' quit? Me—I'll vote for old Abe."

Ben was too young to vote, but he shared the opinions of the others. He was sure that when November came, the Twentieth Maine would go solidly for the tall, sad-faced man in the White House.

In the Confederate ranks there was confidence that the Democrats would win and the war would end before Christmas. Back in the trenches at Petersburg, they were offering the Yankees odds on the result of the election. In spite of short rations and other hardships, this belief kept the Rebels' spirits high.

Before November arrived, however, there was still some hard fighting to be done. Now that they were unable to use the Weldon rail line, the Confederates were hauling supplies to Petersburg by wagon over the Boydton Plank Road, a few miles to the west. They had fortified their position there, and one of their strong points was a fort at a place called Peebles' Farm. It was against this fort that the Fifth Corps moved at the end of September.

Ben and his mates were formed up early on the morning of the thirtieth. The column marched northwest through the scrub pine growth, moving cautiously with a skirmish line out in front. After two or three miles they came to the edge of the woods and looked out across a large area of cleared fields. More than half a mile away on the opposite side were more woods. And there in front of the woods, some distance beyond the farm buildings, was the Confederate line of earthworks, running along a crest of high ground.

The square fort, of earth and logs, stood in the center of the fortified line, with a Rebel flag flying from its top and the muzzles of cannon showing at the embrasures in its front.

The Maine men cast a professional eye at their objective.

" 'Pears like a pretty tough one," Sergeant Gray remarked. "Lots of open ground to cross an' a hand-to-hand fight when we git there. I guess some of us won't be comin' back. Well, their guns are startin' up, so it won't be long now. Load up, boys, an' load careful. Then wait for the bugles."

15

Virginia Autumn

The battle of Peebles' Farm isn't even mentioned in most of the history books, but it was one of the hardest fights in which the Twentieth Maine ever took part.

They waited there while the guns in the fort kept on firing at them. A few shells fell close enough to do some damage, but the Maine men suffered no casualties. It was getting close to noon when the Third Brigade got the order to attack.

The first part of the way wasn't too bad. Ben felt the sweat running down inside his shirt as he moved ahead in line of battle, but he kept going, his eyes on the target they must take. A short way past the farm buildings there was a little ravine that offered some cover. Then they had to climb out on the farther side and start up the slope toward the Confederate line. They were in easy range of the artillery and riflemen now. The Rebel gunners switched to canister, and it was like firing into a tight flock of ducks with a heavy-gauge shotgun. Through the smoke Ben could see men falling, the line thinning out, but those who were left ran harder and yelled their defiance as they went.

Only about half of Company B remained when they reached the abatis of sharpened stakes in front of the fort. They squeezed between the stakes, following the lead of a young lieutenant named Fernald, who seemed to have a charmed life. With dozens of Confederate sharpshooters aiming at his heart, he vaulted over the parapet, revolver in hand, and called on the crew of a field gun to surrender. The other Maine men were close at his heels. Rebel bullets from both sides of them flew wild, killing some of the artillery horses. Then, with more and more Yankees pouring into the redoubt, the Confederate line broke and ran.

The Maine men captured the gun and seventy prisoners, but they had paid a terrible price for victory. The slope was dotted with their dead and wounded. And in the fort itself, Sergeant Gray lay bleeding to death from a dozen canister wounds. Ben and two of his comrades carried him back to the field hospital, but he was dead before they reached it. That was a hard blow to Ben, for Gray had been one of his idols.

That wasn't the end of the day's fighting. In the afternoon some units of the Ninth Corps came past, following the Confederate retreat. Soon the Maine regiment heard a lot of firing off to the northwest. It began coming closer, and then they saw Ninth Corps soldiers streaming back in a hurry. They had run into a hornet's nest of Rebels, sent down to protect the Plank Road.

General Griffin, who commanded the Fifth Corps' First Division, got his men into line of battle along a low, wooded ridge, squarely across the front of the Confederate attackers. It was a thin line, barely stronger than a skirmish line, and at that moment it was under heavy fire from Rebel artillery. But before too much damage was done, Griffin rushed Union guns into place and answered the fire.

A strange thing happened then. Coming toward them through the smoke were masses of men dressed partly in blue. Some had on blue trousers and gray jackets—others just the opposite. But they were firing at the Yankee line as they came.

Officers cried out to the Union soldiers to hold their fire. "Can't you see they're our boys?" one excited captain yelled.

Luckily the veterans knew better. They had seen plenty of Rebels dressed that way, and just in time they gave them a withering blast of rifle fire. When the artillery joined in with canister, the attack faltered, fell back, and soon the Confederates were in full retreat.

The weary Maine men were sober that night. Seven of them were dead and fifty wounded. The only field officer left in the whole Third Brigade was their own Major Ellis Spear. And when he took command of the brigade, a Captain Clark was picked to lead the regiment. Having a captain commanding a regiment wasn't as queer as it seemed, for casualties had cut the Twentieth Maine down almost to company size.

Back in camp along the Weldon Railroad, Ben and his companions had a chance to enjoy the fine weather of a Virginia autumn. As October passed, the nights grew chilly with a hint of coming frost, but the days were bright and golden. Raiding nearby farms, the soldiers found yams for roasting and an occasional well-fattened pig. The scuppernong grapes had ripened in the woods. Ben tried them on one of his rambles and liked their wild, tart-sweet flavor. The taste went well with chestnuts, now popping from their burrs.

It was on the same day that he tried his first persimmon. The yellowish fruit looked tempting enough. Not knowing that persimmons needed a hard frost to make them edible, he picked one and took one bite. That was all he wanted. Hastily he threw the fruit away and went back to camp, his lips still puckered.

Nobody expected this idyllic life to last very long, and of course they were right. The Federal Army still had failed to cut the supply line of the Boydton Plank Road. On the

twenty-seventh of October the Twentieth Maine marched out with a fairly large force to strike in that direction. As was almost sure to happen, it rained hard all day, and a lot of units lost their way in the thick, dark woods.

The battle that followed wasn't one in which the North could take much pride. The scene of it was along a creek called Hatcher's Run, and after pushing the Confederates back at the start, the Yankees ran into such violent counter-attacks that they had to give up the ground they had won. By the time night fell, they were marching back to their bivouacs. The Twentieth Maine had one man killed and two wounded—all for nothing.

Election Day was drawing nearer now. Two days before the voting was to take place, the soldiers heard a general order read. They were to keep in a high state of readiness, since it was feared the Confederates would choose the occasion to attack. On November 8 each qualified voter was to cast his ballot at regimental headquarters as early in the day as possible, then get back to his post.

There was one fact in the Republicans' favor. The war was no longer a losing cause for the North, for Sherman had taken Atlanta and the Confederates seemed to have no army that could stop him. At the same time Sheridan was winning convincingly in the Shenandoah Valley.

The Twentieth Maine voted for Lincoln by an overwhelming majority—138 to 13—and even though the Fifth Corps had been McClellan's favorite command at one time, its vote was heavily Republican.

Results of the election came down to Petersburg by wire, and as each unit heard the news of Lincoln's victory, a great cheer went up. The Confederate soldiers, in their trenches, heard the swelling roar of sound and were puzzled. They yelled across to the men opposite them.

"Hey, Yank!"

"Hi, there, Johnny."

"Don't shoot, Yank."

"All right, Johnny."

"What are you'uns all cheerin' for?"

"Big victory for our side."

"Whar was it at, Yank?"

"All over the North. Old Abe's been re-elected!"

The Rebels, dumfounded at the news, were too glum to answer.

It had taken a good deal of courage for the Army to vote as it had, Ben thought. The choice they were offered was whether to keep on fighting or do what every soldier wanted —go home. And they had chosen to continue the war to a final conclusion.

The regiment got some more action early in December. The whole Fifth Corps started marching south—in the rain, of course. In two days they made forty miles and were some distance south of Stony Creek Station. The Confederates had been shipping supplies up the Weldon Railroad from the south, then hauling them from Stony Creek by wagon around the area where Union forces had cut the line. Now Grant wanted to make even this route impossible, and it was the Fifth Corps' job to destroy the railroad all the way to North Carolina.

The troops made a regular holiday of it. In clear, bright weather after the rain, they stretched their columns down the right-of-way, stacked their rifles, and went to work. Big groups of men dug up the ties and ripped loose the rails. The ties were thrown into huge piles and made splendid bonfires. Then the rails were heated red-hot and twisted around trees to make them unusable. As fast as a division finished one mile-long length of track, it marched on down to a new location. And at nightfall, enjoying the sight of hundreds of blazing fires, they went into bivouac in the fields.

The foragers came in with cattle, pigs, and other food, but while it was cooking, a group of Maine men discovered a haystack concealing twenty-five barrels of applejack. From that time on very little eating and no sleeping was done. The men drank the potent liquor till half the Fifth Corps was tipsy, and the roaring, singing, and fighting had to be subdued by a cavalry detachment. One of the few sober ones, Ben looked back on that night of revelry with considerable disgust.

Before morning a sleet storm began. Many of the drunken soldiers had passed out, lying where they happened to fall, and woke up sheeted with ice. But worse than that, the enemy was arriving in some force. Ben was on picket duty, and before dawn the firing got steadily stronger till he thought the whole camp would be surrounded.

Orders came to pull out, but it took a long time to get the stumbling men on their feet. When at last they did start marching, the chill in the air and the whistle of sniper bullets added to their speed. By night they were twenty miles up the railroad, and the next day they reached the rest of the Army. After that they started building cabins for winter quarters. The location was near the Jerusalem Plank Road, halfway between Petersburg and their old camp on the Weldon line.

That expedition to the south had been costly to the Third Brigade, not in killed or wounded but in stragglers. Some forty-three men were missing, and most of them had probably been captured, too befuddled to keep up with their regiments.

Ben was an old hand at wintering in camp by now. He helped build the snug cabin that would be his home for some months. Loring Hawkes was back after a long time in the hospital, and Ed Morrison had been slightly wounded. So they had their original quartet—Bean, Preble, Hawkes, and Ben. Loring was still pale and weak, but they did their best to feed him up. The country here was better for forage than it had been up above the Rapidan, and thanks to Ike Bean's knack for finding tasty morsels and Martin Preble's cooking, they lived well.

Ben's share of the work was bringing in firewood. It wasn't as easy to get as it had been at first. Sometimes he had to cruise two or three miles to locate a dead pine or oak that he could cut up. And then many trips were required to carry the logs to camp. Sometimes he took along his rifle as well as his ax, and more than once he brought back squirrels or a fat raccoon for the pot.

Mail deliveries were more regular now that the autumn marching and fighting had ended. Every week or two Ben heard from home. His mother, of course, had been overjoyed at learning he was alive and well, though she said her faith had never wavered. At Christmas she sent another box of apples, once more generously wrapped in newspapers. There was also a smaller box that contained maple sugar candy, made with the tender meats of hickory nuts from their own shagbark trees.

Unfortunately, most of Company B was present when Ben opened the package, and the candy was soon gone. But the apples and the newspapers continued to make the occupants of the cabin happy till after the New Year of 1865 had begun.

In many ways, Ben thought sadly, the Twentieth Maine was a different regiment now. Out of its original enrollment, not more than two hundred were left. Wounds, illness, death, and capture had drained away the rest. And the hundreds of new recruits added in the last months of 1864 seemed like a totally different breed. All were draftees, with a few bounty men. None of them had had any military training, and they lacked the sense of duty that Ben had seen evidenced so many times among the veteran troops. A few unprincipled youths were given to stealing from their comrades. Others never did any work that they could get out of doing. A small number, Ben admitted, would some day make good soldiers. But whether the regiment would ever again have the same valiant fighting qualities it had shown in earlier battles was an open question.

The winter was far from over when they went into action again. Early in February, on a cold, snowy day, the Fifth Corps, including their own Third Brigade, started its attack on the Rebel outposts guarding the supply roads.

Even before they reached Hatcher's Run, they were in thick woods and had to plow through swamps and thickets and wade icy streams. They struggled on past the river, and by late afternoon the brigade ran into a Confederate line near Dabney's Mill. There wasn't too much resistance, and they chased the gray-clad soldiers back through the woods for another half mile.

Then, all of a sudden, the Maine veterans knew why it had been so easy. In front of them were strong entrenchments and a stronger Rebel line, waiting for the Yankees to walk into their trap. In another moment a heavy force of Confederates came charging out, and the green recruits turned tail like so many scared rabbits. There were too few seasoned men left to stand the charge. The rout that followed was one of the few disgraces ever suffered by the Twentieth Maine. Before it was over, the whole brigade was in flight, panting through the tangled brush. Little knots of Union men would try to make a stand, fire a volley or two, then find themselves unsupported and have to run again.

Colonel Gilmore, who had come back from service in Washington to take command of the Twentieth Maine, tried in vain to rally his rattled recruits and was overrun by the Rebel charge. For a matter of minutes he was a prisoner. Then, in the general confusion, he got away from his captors and succeeded in reaching the Union lines. The disorderly retreat had stopped when the fleeing Yankees got to a ridge where batteries of their own artillery were mounted. Canister and round shot soon drove the Confederates off.

Ben and the other veterans had borne themselves as well as any soldiers could. But they always hung their heads in shame when Dabney's Mill was mentioned. There had been twenty-four casualties in the regiment during the affair. Far worse than that was the hurt to their pride. Even the rawest rookies ached for a chance to redeem themselves.

The Federal lines had at last been extended as far as Hatcher's Run, and there Ben and his tentmates built a fresh hut, where they would wait out the rest of the winter.

16

Another Spring

There came mild days in March, with frogs piping their spring song in the hollows—a full month earlier than in northern New England. Little by little the Twentieth Maine was pulling itself together. The worst of the recruits were weeded out by desertion or court-martial, and those who remained were learning obedience to orders. Still smarting under the taunts of other units, they burned now with a desire to show what they could really do.

One event pleased the men of Company B. Their own captain, Walter Morrill, now promoted to lieutenant colonel, took over the command of the regiment. Gilmore had returned to Washington, and Ellis Spear had been made a full colonel and moved to division headquarters. To the men who had fought under Morrill at Gettysburg and in the Wilderness, there would never be a more popular or trusted officer.

By this time, the veteran enlisted men realized what the spring campaign could mean. If ever the war was to be won, now was their opportunity, for the Confederates were stretched thin, trying to protect their lines of supply all the way from Richmond and Petersburg around to the South Side Railroad. What was coming, the Yankees were sure, was another strong flanking attack to the west.

The army that was to do the attacking was a mixed force of cavalry and infantry under the command of General Phil Sheridan himself. The Maine men got their first look at the famous cavalry leader in mid-March. He wasn't as impressive to see as some of his subordinates, like the flamboyant General Custer with his blond ringlets, but he did have a look of power under leash. Sheridan was short, broad-shouldered, and a little stooped. His hair was clipped close to his bullet head, and a thick mustache gave him a ferocious appearance. His uniform looked worn and dusty, but his horse was a big black charger—one of the finest Ben had ever seen.

On the twenty-ninth of March, the Fifth Corps was in marching order early in the morning. Joshua Chamberlain, once the Twentieth Maine's colonel, was back in the saddle after the terrible wounds he had suffered in the first attack on Petersburg, and he led the First Brigade of the First Division. His old comrades of the Third Brigade were close behind, and they would be proud of him that day.

The division moved through the woods northward along the Quaker Road, knowing they would soon meet with a stiff defense. It was waiting for them at Gravelly Run. There the Confederates had destroyed the bridge and entrenched themselves on the farther bank. With Chamberlain in the lead, the Union men waded across through hip-deep water under fire, charged the Rebel line, and broke it. Then began a chase of a mile or more up the Quaker Road until the retreating Confederates reached a second line and reinforcements. There they turned to fight, sheltered behind stout breastworks.

Chamberlain gave his men barely time to catch their breath, then sent them in to attack. With fixed bayonets his brigade went up the road at a run, straight toward the middle of the Rebel line. The Maine men saw their former leader ride his white horse in a charge that took him out in front of the foot soldiers. Suddenly the horse reared up, just as a sharpshooter's bullet came toward its rider. The shot ripped through the neck of the horse and into Chamberlain's arm and body. And while they both stood there bleeding, the attack swept on past them.

The men on the right side of the road hit the trenches first and were thrown back by intense musketry fire. In a moment they were running away in confusion, and it looked like another rout. But to the amazement of all who saw it, Chamberlain suddenly jerked himself erect in the saddle, urged his wounded mount to a run, and rode into the midst of the retreating soldiers. They stopped, turned, and went back cheering to hit the line once more. This time, supported by the Twentieth Maine, they fought their way up to the breastworks in a fierce hand-to-hand battle.

General Griffin came riding up, helped Chamberlain off the dying horse, and sent more brigades into the attack. "If you can hold on there for ten minutes," he shouted, "I'll get artillery up to help!"

So the Yankees hung on, fighting with bayonets and clubbed rifles, and Griffin was as good as his word. In ten minutes shells were whistling over their heads from a Union battery. The Rebels wilted under the fire and moved out, retreating toward still another line of entrenchments to the north. The victory opened the way for an assault on the main Confederate defenses along the White Oak Road.

For his bravery in action, Joshua Chamberlain was immediately given a brevet commission as major general—an honor all the Maine men heartily approved. Somewhere, during those vital ten minutes while they held on, waiting for the guns, the wounded Chamberlain had found another horse. For a long time the men in Company B argued hotly whether the one he had been riding was the seventh or the eighth that had been shot under him in the course of the war.

"Anyhow," Ike Bean pronounced, "if I was a hoss, I'd be mighty skittish about lettin' Josh Chamberlain git on my back. Trouble is, he's allus up front where the bullets is thickest."

*   *   *

All that night the rain came down in torrents. While the wounded lay on the ground under ponchos, the rest of the Twentieth Maine spent the hours of darkness digging entrenchments that filled up with water almost as soon as they were finished. At last they got a few hours of rest in their rain-drenched blankets. Nobody slept much, and at daybreak they were ordered out to prepare for battle once more.

The Rebels had dug in on a line about a quarter of a mile to the north. The Third Brigade made the assault on this line shortly after noon. It was still raining, but they succeeded in carrying the trenches and stayed there to fight off the Confederate counterattacks. By the time darkness fell, there was no way to tell that they were Federal soldiers, for their blue uniforms were completely plastered with red Virginia mud.

At least the Twentieth Maine had one thing to be grateful for that night. A force from the Second Corps moved in to relieve them, and they marched off to the left to rejoin the rest of the Fifth Corps.

By morning the sun was shining, and things seemed a little less miserable. Their division was back in the woods in reserve, and it looked as if they might get a day of rest. Up ahead of them, the other two divisions of the Fifth Corps were going to attack Confederate positions on the White Oak Road. The Maine men sat around and enjoyed the sunshine while the usual roar of battle drifted back to them.

The trouble was that the sounds kept coming louder and closer. Soon they could even hear the dreaded Rebel yell, and they quit eating hardtack and jumped for their rifles. As the bugles called, they formed up, and the whole brigade went forward at the double-quick to a ridge that looked down on Gravelly Run. There they saw the other divisions coming toward them in headlong flight.

The line of Confederates was close on their heels, whooping and firing as they ran. Then the Third Brigade opened up with a storm of rifle fire, and the Rebel charge began to break. Union field guns did the rest. A band started to play, and the sound of the music put new heart in the retreating Yankees. By the time they turned around, the Confederates were stopped in their tracks.

However, the Fifth Corps had lost some ground in the fight, and their honor demanded it be recovered. General Warren came to Chamberlain, asking him to lead a fresh attack. And in spite of his wounds and weakness, the Maine man got up from the pile of straw where he had been lying, was helped onto a horse, and led his troops in a tremendous charge that drove the Rebels back well beyond the White Oak Road.

Meanwhile, five or six miles south at Dinwiddie Court House, Sheridan's cavalry had gotten into difficulties. The Maine soldiers could hear heavy firing coming from that direction, and they soon knew the Fifth Corps was about to spend another night without sleep. In pitchy darkness they started to the relief of Sheridan. The enemy was still there, close to the White Oak Road, and some brigades were left to hold them off while the rest, including the Twentieth Maine, marched southward. They were on a narrow woods road, so dark that men kept bumping into each other. When they had been going for an hour or so, an order came from somewhere telling them to turn around and march back. They grumbled and swore but did as they were told.

The nightmarish expedition wasn't over, however. A couple of miles north, they met the First Brigade, with the redoubtable General Chamberlain riding ahead. After holding the Rebels on the White Oak Road, he had been sent down to reinforce the Third Brigade. The Maine men had spent a bad twenty-four hours fighting and slogging through the wet woods, but they were cheered by the sight of their hero. They would follow Josh Chamberlain anywhere. So once more they swung around and retraced their steps.

At dawn they halted, for a mile away a big force of cavalry was coming up the road. It wasn't until the early sun shone on blue uniforms that they realized they weren't facing Confederates. Soon Sheridan himself came galloping up, his face like a thundercloud. He was angry because he had been driven back by Fitzhugh Lee's cavalry and Pickett's division of infantry, and he was putting the blame on the Fifth Corps for letting him down.

A few of the Maine men could overhear the remarks he made to Chamberlain.

"Huh!" Martin Preble snorted under his breath. "That puffed-up hoss-soldier! Might think he figgered we'd all stayed safe in camp, playin' mumblety-peg! If he was half the gin'ral Ol' Josh is, we'd ha' won the war 'fore now."

The morning was fair and cool, and the bedraggled, tired men of the Twentieth Maine at last sat down to a breakfast of coffee and hardtack. Perhaps, Ben thought, they would get a little breathing spell—even a whole day of rest. But within two hours, he knew his hopes were blasted. Field officers of the Fifth Corps had been at a conference with Sheridan, and as soon as they returned, a rumor ran through the ranks that a big battle was coming.

The Confederates had pulled back to the north, five or six miles from Dinwiddie Court House. Now they were strongly entrenched at a place called Five Forks, where a number of roads met. This time Sheridan wanted the infantry to attack the center and left of the enemy line while the cavalry galloped around to the west and turned their right flank.

The Fifth Corps got into marching order early in the afternoon, and by four o'clock they were in line of battle near Gravelly Run Church, a little south of the Confederate position. They made an impressive sight as they moved forward. Ben's heart quickened with pride to be part of that powerful array.

Sheridan had drawn a map of the operation for General Warren, but as it turned out later, the map was wrong. It showed the Rebel lines extending farther to the east than was actually the case. Two divisions of the corps were to lead the way northward, with Griffin's First Division in support.

The Confederate trenches were hidden by woods as the attackers advanced, and they had no way of knowing they would miss the defense line entirely. Skirmishers from the Rebel ranks were making plenty of noise in their front, however, so they pushed on, driving these scattered defenders farther and farther back. Soon they were across the White Oak Road and plowing on into woods that grew thicker and wilder as they went.

Once more it was General Chamberlain who discovered what had happened. He heard a lot of firing off to his left and rode to a bit of high, open ground where he could look in that direction. To his amazement he saw the end of the Confederate line being attacked by Ayres' division. It was actually well to the south of where the other two divisions had gone. They had completely flanked the Rebels and were now in their rear!

Chamberlain led two brigades back to attack the trenches from the north, and at once Bartlett, in command of the Third Brigade, did the same thing. The Twentieth Maine, along with the First Michigan, wheeled left and hurried south through the woods. Coming over a hill, they saw the rear of the main Confederate line below them, its soldiers busy watching for attackers in their front. So quietly did the two regiments descend the slope that they took the Rebels utterly by surprise. Hundreds of the men in gray threw down their arms. Suddenly the Yankees had so many prisoners that they hardly knew what to do with them.

Ben and his squadmates were congratulating themselves on an almost bloodless victory when a Confederate soldier suddenly picked up a rifle and shouted, "We kin whip you'uns yet!" With that he fired point-blank and shot down a captain of the First Michigan. Ike Bean was the nearest man to him. Without a second's hesitation, he laid the Rebel out with the butt of his musket, and immediately the battle started in earnest. The two Union regiments, heavily outnumbered, had to fight hand-to-hand, right in the enemy trench.

It was one of the fiercest, bloodiest engagements Ben had ever been in. Things were going badly for the Maine men when more regiments came roaring in to help. Then bugles sounded the charge, and a big detachment of Federal cavalry rode up. So that April Fool's Day ended at last. The Yankee forces had turned a stupid mistake into one of their biggest victories. They had practically wiped out Pickett's famous division and taken some five thousand prisoners.

Sadly, by the light of candles, the Maine soldiers searched

the scene of the battle that night, found their dead comrades, and buried them under a big oak tree. One of the bodies was that of the giant Ed Morrison, back in action in spite of his wound. During the conflict they had seen him swinging his clubbed musket like an ax, felling the enemy all around him.

So Ben had lost another of his closest friends. He found only one comfort in the events of the past two days. It seemed to him that Lee's dreaded Army of Northern Virginia was beginning to fall apart. The Confederates still fought with great bravery, but there were fewer of them, and Grant's forces were growing stronger every day. The war that had once seemed destined to go on forever now looked as if it might be nearing its end.

17

Appomattox

The victory at Five Forks had opened the way to the last supply line remaining to the Rebels—the South Side Railroad. On the morning of April 2 the Fifth Corps marched across country to capture that vital link.

Just as Ben's regiment reached the tracks, a cloud of smoke was sighted off to the east. Their commander, Lieutenant Colonel Morrill, took one look and ordered the men to barricade the track.

"Train coming!" he yelled. "Get logs, on the double!"

It took only a couple of minutes to fell a big tree and drag it across the rails. Then, around a curve, came a battered little Confederate locomotive, puffing furiously as it hauled twelve cars up the slight grade.

The engineer was almost on top of the barricade before he could brake to a stop. Instantly there were Maine soldiers all over the train, disarming the guards and opening the doors of the boxcars.

"By thunder!" cried Ike Bean. "It's a load o' Yankee prisoners!"

Ben leaped aboard, pushing through the crowd of living skeletons inside. "Rocky!" he was yelling. "Joe Sampson! Anybody here seen him?"

His voice was lost in the hysterical cheering and crying of the liberated prisoners. They were being helped to the ground by the men of the Twentieth Maine. In a few minutes cook fires were lit, and food was given to the starving captives. It shocked the soldiers to look at their gaunt frames and watch the way they wolfed down their rations.

Meanwhile, Ben was keeping up his search. In the last car of the train he finally came upon a thin, bearded ghost of a man, lying on an old burlap bag. He could scarcely believe it was his friend until the weak voice spoke his name.

"My gosh, Joe!" Ben choked. "Wh-what's happened to you? You been sick?"

"Some." Sampson tried to smile. "Mostly just couldn't git enough to eat. Boy, I'm sure s'prised to see you. That night, when I heard them guards firin', I thought you was gone."

Gently Ben picked up the wasted figure, once so strong and sturdy.

"Here!" he called from the car door. "Company B this way! One of our own men's come home!"

Ike Bean and Martin Preble helped lift Sampson down. "There's some ambulance wagons loadin' up," said Ike. "Let's get him back to a hospital. First, though, I aim to feed him."

They brought a pannikin of stew, and Joe managed, with some difficulty, to eat a little. "My teeth," he croaked. "Used to crack walnuts with 'em. Now they're loose from scurvy."

"Well, thunderation!" Preble exclaimed. "Vegetables is what you need. We'll find some an' send 'em to the hospital. Why, Rocky, you used to be one o' the huskiest men in the regiment!"

"Thanks, boys," Sampson murmured. "Back there at Belle Isle, I didn't have no heart fer stayin' alive. Now I got some reason to git well."

The last of the ambulances was about to pull out. They helped the medical corps men load their old comrade in and made sure that he rode comfortably. As the vehicle creaked away, Ben felt a great weight lift from his heart. For months he had had a feeling of guilt about running off and leaving Sampson on the prison island.

That was the last train the Rebels tried to run on the South Side Railroad. The next day a Union officer came galloping up, bringing great news. The men of the Twentieth Maine heard him shouting it as he rode by. Petersburg had fallen! The Confederate Government in Richmond was getting out as fast as possible!

The veterans found it hard to believe. After four dismal years of mud and slaughter, it was too good to be true. Only when their own colonel confirmed the report did they stop scoffing and begin to cheer.

But the marching and fighting weren't over yet, as they soon discovered. The indomitable Lee was pulling his men out of the lines, it was true, but only to rush them around the Yankees and get them down to North Carolina. There he hoped to join his forces with those of General Joe Johnston. If he succeeded, the South would still have a formidable army in the field.

"It 'pears to me," said Ike Bean, "that we better git our runnin' shoes on. If I know the signs, we're goin' to have to march faster'n we ever did before if we aim to stop Lee."

The Second and Sixth Corps, ordered out of the Petersburg lines, hurried to join the Fifth Corps near Jetersville, but they didn't stay long. By April 6 they were sent north to follow on Lee's heels as he pushed westward. And the Fifth Corps, including the Twentieth Maine, moved due west in the wake of Sheridan's cavalry. Ben and his mates tightened up their belts, lightened their packs, and hustled along the narrow roads with every ounce of strength they had. They knew if they went fast enough they could finish the war.

Their line of march ran south of Lee's and roughly parallel with it. The route crossed streams where they had to wade through water up to their armpits, holding rifles and cartridge boxes high overhead to keep them dry. And again it led through thick woods. When one section of the column was held up, struggling through the brush, the men would close the gap by trotting at double time to catch up as soon as they were free.

Off to the north, as they marched, they could hear a continuous distant rumble of artillery. The Army of Northern Virginia was now hard pressed, fighting rear-guard actions against the pursuing Second and Sixth Corps and being cut up on the flank by cavalry attacks. Word came that the Rebel soldiers were living on nothing but a few grains of parched corn and were dropping along the road by hundreds from starvation and exhaustion.

"Mebbe they've got it tough," Martin Preble panted, as Company B hurried on. "But I figger we ain't so much better off. My stummick's tied up in knots from short rations right now."

On April 8 there was no food left in the knapsacks of the Twentieth Maine, and they had to make a march of nearly thirty miles that day. They didn't succeed, but it wasn't hunger that stopped them. It was a regiment of Union artillery that tried to roll right over them. The woods road was narrow, and the snorting horses and heavy gun carriages forced the infantry off into the brush. It was more than the tired, hungry soldiers could stand. Horses were knocked down by musket butts, drivers used their whips, and even some of the officers got involved in violent altercations.

By the time the fight calmed down, the Maine men had

fallen a long way behind the rest of the column. They went stumbling on, and finally, at two o'clock the next morning, they caught up with their division. With groans of relief, they threw themselves down to rest. But at that moment, the order came for the other two regiments to start on again.

The Twentieth Maine had been on its feet nearly twenty-four hours. The men were as near total exhaustion as they had ever been, and some of them simply could not get up after their few minutes of rest. Loring Hawkes was one of these.

"You fellers go ahead," he panted. "I'm too beat to stand up, let alone march. I'll do my best to ketch up later."

Ben, Ike, and Martin fell in with their company and went on, moving like sleepwalkers. When dawn broke, there were only seventy-five men of the regiment left in the column.

Lieutenant Colonel Morrill rode his jaded horse back along the line. "Boys," he told them, "I know what you've been through, but I've got good news. Just six miles ahead, there's plenty of food waiting for you. It's a little place they call Appomattox Station, and I promise that when you get there, you'll rest and eat."

They believed him. Morrill had never let them down. With the thought of food luring them on, they plodded forward, mile after weary mile. But something happened before they received the promised rations. As they staggered up to Appomattox Station, they could hear a sound of heavy firing off to the north. Several officers from Sheridan's staff halted the Fifth Corps marchers, turned them toward the right, and told their field officers they were needed to support Sheridan's cavalry, now squarely across the path of Lee's advance.

The roar of battle came louder with every yard they covered. The Union horse-artillery was barking, but its sound was drowned by the thunder of heavier enemy guns. Then, as they drew nearer, they could hear the rattle and snap of musketry and carbine fire.

Ben had even forgotten his hunger now. The Twentieth Maine was coming in from the southeast and was in the front rank of the Fifth Corps column. Just ahead of him, he saw the color-bearers shake out their battle flags, and at that moment sunlight came through the clouds to shine on the tattered banners. A kind of exultation made him tremble at the sight.

Then across the front of the advancing infantry battle lines, Sheridan himself went galloping by on his great black horse, followed by an aide who carried the famous swallow-tailed pennon. This was Phil Sheridan's moment of triumph. With solid infantry to back him, the hard-eyed general knew he had Lee stopped.

The Maine men hadn't yet sighted the enemy. Shells were falling around them but doing little damage as they climbed a low ridge toward a farmhouse and outbuildings. Suddenly a shell burst in the farm's henhouse. A feathery cloud of chickens went squawking and fluttering almost under their feet, and for the moment all discipline was forgotten. Ben and his comrades rushed around grabbing at the frightened birds, their weariness left behind.

It took some sharp orders from their officers to get them back in line of battle, but several soldiers had chickens hanging from their belts. They marched on, over the crest of the hill. And there, across the width of an open field, they saw the Army they had fought so long. First there were skirmishers behind shallow earthworks. Behind them, higher up the opposite slope, was the long, grim line of gray uniforms and red battle flags.

The men of the Twentieth Maine drew a long breath like a sigh and started forward. Ben had a strange feeling about this fight. It would, he thought, be the last one of the war, and what a shame it was that men must die on this day of final victory!

Any moment now, as they advanced, the rifle fire would come whistling to meet them. They set their jaws hard and kept their line, every man expecting to see the red flash from Rebel muskets.

There was an orchard back of the Confederate line from where their field gun batteries were firing. Suddenly something white was waving there. It came moving on, through the infantry, then past the skirmishers. It was a white flag, carried by a rider on horseback.

The artillery fire stopped, and there was a great silence over the field between the two armies. Cavalry horses, champing and pawing, made the only sound except for a murmur of amazement that ran along the line of halted troops.

Other white flags kept coming toward the Union commanders. Then the word was passed. Lee was surrendering! A tremendous cheer went up, and men hugged each other, danced, yelled, and threw caps and knapsacks into the air.

As they soon discovered, the surrender hadn't actually happened yet. Regimental officers passed the word to their troops that a truce was declared until one o'clock that afternoon. So the Maine men sat down where they were, made sure their rifles were loaded, and waited to see what would come next.

It was an uneasy time. The truce was nearly broken when some impetuous Rebel fired at Sheridan as he rode toward a meeting of the general staff. And the Yankees, still hungry, growled and fingered their guns. Finally one o'clock

arrived. It looked as if they would be fighting again at any moment.

Then Ben saw a little group of Confederate officers riding closer through their lines. One of them was a fine-looking man with a gray beard, who sat very straight on his grayish-white charger. It was Ben's first sight of the South's great general.

"That's Robert E. Lee himself!" Ike Bean said almost reverently. "An' he's ridin' ol' Traveler!"

Lee was nearly as much of a legend among the Yankee veterans as in his own Army of Northern Virginia. He had out-guessed, outmaneuvered, and outfought them in a hundred battles, large and small. That he had finally come to the end of the road was hard for them to comprehend.

A few minutes later they caught a glimpse of General Grant, riding in the same direction. The contrast was noticeable. The leader of the Union forces wore no gold braid on his mud-spattered uniform, and he sat slouched in the saddle.

He paused when he was just in front of Ben's regiment and glanced toward the village that clustered about Appomattox Court House. "Is General Lee there yet?" he asked a Union general. "Very well. Let's go up."

The conference took a considerable time, and while it was in progress, a few Yankee soldiers got up, left their rifles, and wandered over to the Confederate lines. On an impulse, Ben went, too. He greeted several of the ragged soldiers with a grin, swapped anecdotes about Peebles' Farm and Five Forks, and gave one man the end of a plug of tobacco he had in his pocket.

"By the way," he asked, "any Carolina soldiers around here? I was thinkin' of a young feller 'bout my age by the name of Ellington—John Ellington."

The man shook his head, but another had heard the words. "Jack Ellington?" he asked. "I knew him, but he's daid now. Got kilt back at Petersburg when the big mine blew up. How'd you git to know him, Yank?"

"It was when I was a fresh recruit, way back in the spring o' sixty-three. We were guardin' the fords along the Rappahannock, an' I used to go swimmin' with him. Sorry to hear he's gone. I liked him a lot."

"Ain't got any sort o' rations on ye, have ye, Yank?" the Confederates kept asking. "Us'ns ain't had mo'n a mouthful fo' nigh onto a week."

They looked it, too. Except on Belle Isle, Ben had never seen men so emaciated. He had to tell them he had no food, but he was ashamed to admit he had gone hungry for only two days.

Soon the visiting Northerners were called back to their own lines. With some sternness they were told that until the truce became final, they were to stay vigilant. For a while, as darkness settled over the fields, pickets went out to keep their watch. Then they came straggling back. By midnight practically all the soldiers of both armies were sleeping quietly in their blankets, only a few yards apart, under the gentle rain.

18

The Surrender

That historic day had been Palm Sunday, April 9, 1865. On Monday morning the men of the Twentieth Maine knew the terms of surrender had been agreed upon. To the veterans they seemed fair enough—not harsh but just. The entire Southern Army was to lay down its arms and turn over all public property to the victors. That included artillery, horses, flags, and small arms. Only those men who owned their horses would be allowed to take them home to work the fields. Grant, it was said, had refused to take Lee's sword.

Shortly, a long train of commissary wagons came toiling up the road from Appomattox Station, bringing enough hardtack and bacon to feed both armies. After that everybody was in a cheerful mood.

The actual ceremony of surrender didn't take place until April 12. General Joshua Chamberlain had asked to be transferred back to the command of his old brigade—the Third, which included the Maine men. Now they lined up proudly, happy to be serving directly under their favorite field officer once more. And that very morning they learned that Chamberlain's command was to represent all the Union forces during the laying down of arms!

The old, worn uniforms had been brushed, the muddy

boots cleaned. Every man formed up for the parade with eyes front and shoulders squared. They marched into the little town and lined up along both sides of the main street, from Appomattox Creek nearly to the Court House.

Not far away they could see the gray-clad troops. They were just breaking camp—their last camp. Soon they started forming ranks, and slowly, leaden-footed, they began their march.

Chamberlain, at that moment, did a generous thing. He sent orders along the lines that the Confederates were to receive the marching salute.

Later on he was to be bitterly criticized for his action by politicians in the North. But in his own words, heartily approved by the Twentieth Maine, these were his reasons:

"Before us," he said, "in proud humiliation, stood the embodiment of manhood: men whom neither toils nor sufferings, nor the fact of death, nor disaster, nor hopelessness could bend from their resolve; standing before us now, thin, worn and famished, but erect, and with eyes looking level into ours, waking memories that bound us together as no other bond. Was not such manhood to be welcomed back into a Union so tested and so assured?"

When the head of the Confederate column reached the beginning of the Third Brigade's line, there came a bugle call. In rhythmic order the Yankee soldiers slapped their rifle butts and lifted their rifles to "carry" position.

General John B. Gordon, riding at the head of the Rebel march, heard the sound and looked up, astonished. Ben saw the gloom go from his face. He wheeled his horse and pulled back on the bridle till the animal reared high. At the same time, he returned the salute by touching his boot toe with the point of his sword. Then he swung about and ordered his own troops to port arms as the Yankees had done.

Soon commands rang out from the Confederate officers.

"Halt! Front face! Stack arms!" The gray ranks faced the Third Brigade, stacked their muskets and cartridge boxes, and laid down their colors.

So it went for hours, as the Confederates passed, brigade after brigade. Nobody in the Union ranks felt like cheering. Every so often Federal Army wagons came up and carted away the growing stacks of arms.

Ben Everett, watching the surrender through those long hours, felt closer to the beaten Rebels than to some of his own people. They had suffered the same hard marching and digging and fighting, the same hunger and weariness. When he thought of fat, loud-mouthed profiteers at home, these men before him seemed more like friends and kinfolk.

It was growing dark when the last of the Confederate columns had passed. Their formations broke up into little groups, or pairs, or men all alone, wandering off into the dusk. They were no longer an army—just a crowd of sad-faced people, anxious to start walking the long miles home. When they had gone, somebody set fire to the piles of cartridges left in the street. They flared fiercely, with the familiar stench of gunpowder, and finally burned out in the deepening dark.

*   *   *

The war wasn't ended yet for the Twentieth Maine. They still had a lot of work to do, cleaning up the Confederate camp. Many regiments, they found, had simply dumped their muskets there and gone off without bothering to join in the formal surrender. All this abandoned equipment had to be gathered up and turned over to the Government.

Meanwhile, Ben and his fellows were cold and hungry. Most of them had thrown away their blankets on the last hard march to Appomattox, and with the bridges destroyed, no food or supplies could reach them by wagon. The rations they had received earlier had been shared generously with the Rebels.

They tried foraging but found the surrounding country stripped of food. A few men were so desperate that they dug up kernels of corn, scattered where the cavalry had fed its horses. Washed off and parched in a fire, these grains made poor fare, but they were better than nothing.

It was chilly and a heavy rain was drenching them when they left Appomattox on the fifteenth of April. But it cleared as they marched, and when they got to Farmville, the sun was out. Better yet, they found wagons there with rations and mail.

Ben's spirits rose as he munched hardtack and drank coffee. Then came news that made them sink again. A pall of gloom settled over all the troops, for they heard that President Lincoln was dead! Watching a play in the theater, he had been shot by an assassin and died before morning.

The report stunned them. It was true enough, but along with it came wild rumors that a group of Southern sympathizers in Washington were plotting to wipe out the whole Government in the same way. For a while some of the more hotheaded Yankees swore they would kill the first Rebel they saw. That night a double guard was put around their camp, for the officers were afraid they might try to take revenge on the local people.

The Maine men were in a calmer frame of mind when their march was halted, four days later, to show respect for the dead President's funeral. It was being held in Washington at that hour, and military units, wherever they were, paused in reverence. Ben helped to hang black crape on the headquarters tent. Then they stood in formation while the minute guns boomed and the band played a solemn dirge. Their grief was deep and real.

With no reason for haste, the Twentieth Maine marched toward Petersburg. Their pace was leisurely, and they could camp in comfort every night. Ample rations were supplemented by gifts of hoe cakes and fine fresh milk from the many freed slaves they met along the road.

The Negroes would line up to greet the advancing column, laughing, cheering, and singing spirituals in their rich voices. In return, the regimental bands would play march music, and everybody enjoyed the exchange. It was May 3 when the Fifth Corps approached Petersburg. For miles they threaded the fortifications where the late enemy had defended the city so bravely for so many months. Petersburg itself bore scars of the long bombardment, though the houses had never been deliberately shelled.

The weather was oppressively hot when they marched through Richmond, and the men were grateful to some of the ladies of the town who treated them to pitchers of cold water. Curious, they stared at the ruined buildings as they marched along. Fires that had been set by the retreating Rebels to destroy ammunition and supplies had gotten out of hand. A great many houses were gutted by the flames. Yet there was still a kind of tragic beauty about this city that had once been the proud capital of the Confederacy.

Ben pointed out to his companions the route he had followed in his escape from Belle Isle. The island itself lay abandoned now, with grass and bushes beginning to cover its scars with green.

"Gosh!" said Martin Preble. "You mean you swum that river above the falls? Looks mighty dangerous to me."

"I guess it was." Ben chuckled. "Didn't have time to think much about it, though. All I wanted was to git out o' range o' those bullets."

Heading northward, they began to pass battlefields that

stirred sad memories. "This," they would tell one another, "was the place where Billy Gilman got it. Remember—we buried him under that old pine yonder."

There were many more such spots, as they crossed the Chickahominy, the Pamunkey, and the Mattapony. When they came to think of it, there were more men of the original regiment lying in the fields and swamps of Virginia than remained in the ranks.

Once, when they camped for the night near the Pamunkey River, General Chamberlain's horse pawed the dirt and leaves and uncovered some human bones. There were belt buckles and other metal objects with them. The Maine men recognized initials cut on some of these and identified the skeletons. They belonged to comrades reported missing in action, way back in the days when the division had fought under McClellan. Carefully the bones were packed in empty cracker boxes and shipped home for burial.

The final day of their northward march was the least pleasant of their whole journey. There was mud on the roads that made the footing slippery, and in the afternoon came a heavy thunderstorm. A bolt of lightning hit their column, dancing along the rifle muzzles and killing one soldier. Even the smallest streams were swollen and deep, and the corduroy roads had holes that let a man's foot slip through to the knee. No orders came to stop the march till after midnight. The story went that two corps commanders had a bet on, each trying to beat the other to Washington. Whether it was true or not, they were roundly cursed by the rank and file, trying to sleep in the sopping wet woods.

They were mud-covered, tired, and dejected when they got to Arlington Heights early the next day. There was a fog hiding the city of Washington, but it began to thin as they watched. Soon the sun shone down on white buildings, and they felt that at last they were coming home.

The whole Fifth Corps went into bivouac there on the heights across the Potomac to wait for the Grand Review, which would be held May 23. Many other soldiers were there alongside them, including the tough Westerners who had marched up from Georgia under Sherman. Sherman's "bummers" were a wild-looking lot, bearded, with long, uncut hair and sunburned faces, dressed in outlandish combinations of blue and gray. Most of them wore wide-brimmed slouch hats, and their boots still had the clay of the deep South on them.

These veterans from Illinois, Wisconsin, and Iowa had a high opinion of themselves and a very poor one of the Army of the Potomac. One night a gang of half a dozen of them came swaggering over to the row of tents that housed Company B. They appeared just as Ben, Ike, Martin, and Loring had finished eating and were putting away their utensils.

"Huh!" A big fellow from Michigan sneered. "Look at the fancy fixin's these city slickers have got! 'Pears like you Easterners never had to rough it much. All you done was lay in trenches while we was marchin' a couple o' thousan' mile an' winnin' the war. Hey, Bije—take a look at this young 'un! Skin as pale as a girl's!"

He laid a brawny hand on Loring Hawkes and dragged him out in the open. The young farmer had regained some of his strength after Appomattox, but he was still far from well. Ben stepped forward.

"Leave him be," he told the Westerner. "He's been wounded an' sick."

"Who's tellin' me to leave him be?" asked the big fellow belligerently. "Git out o' my way, sonny!"

His shove drove Ben back a step but gave him more room to maneuver. The young soldier was angry now. He swung a blow from his hip that landed flush on the Michigander's jaw and knocked him flat. Then he had his hands full, for the rest of the Sherman men rushed into the fracas. Ike and Martin were flailing around them at the intruders, and other Company B soldiers arrived on the run. In something under thirty seconds, the Westerners were on the ground, with irate Maine men standing over them.

"Trouble with you fellers," Ike Bean panted, "is you never had to fight anybody but home guards an' bushwhackers. Never come up against Robert E. Lee an' licked him, like we did. Next time you come visitin' the Twentieth Maine, you better show some respect."

The hard feelings between the two armies continued, with occasional outbreaks, through the rest of the time they were there. Some of the regiments in the Army of the Potomac had drawn flashy new uniforms and were inclined to strut about in them. The Fifth Corps veterans decided they would rather look as if they had been to war, so they simply cleaned their clothes as best they could, shined up their boots, and kept their rifles gleaming. At least, they felt, they would look more military than Sherman's bummers.

The morning of the Grand Review dawned clear and cool. The buglers had called the Fifth Corps out very early, and by sunup they were on the march across the Potomac and into Washington. Not far from the Capitol, they halted, waiting for their turn in the order of march. Ben had never seen so many soldiers—or so many civilians—in his life.

At last General Griffin and his staff mounted their horses to lead the Fifth Corps up Pennsylvania Avenue. General Chamberlain was helped into his saddle, heading the ranks of the First Division. Behind him flew the old white flag with the red Maltese cross—the famous division colors. The Third Brigade led the way in a wide front that filled the whole breadth of the avenue. Their lines were straight as a plumb-line, and the men swung along in the route step, rifles on their right shoulders.

As they reached the turn near the Treasury Building, there was another bugle call—"Prepare for Review." Then the bands began to play as they marched in step with the music. The tune they played was the familiar "John Brown's Body," but it had new words now, written, Ben had heard, by a New England woman named Howe. It was called "The Battle Hymn of the Republic," and its stirring refrain, "Glory, glory, hallelujah!" was something to lift men's hearts.

Both sides of the street were packed with people as far as the eye could see, and red, white, and blue bunting flew from every building. There was noise, too—a mounting wave of cheering that almost smothered the sound of the bands. In the distance artillery was firing constantly in a series of salutes.

Then at last they approached the President's reviewing stand. Andrew Johnson was there, surrounded by members of the Cabinet and all the war's famous generals. There was a ruffle of drums, and the colors were dipped in homage to the Chief Executive. Ben felt one regret that was shared, he knew, by many other soldiers at that moment. If only Abe Lincoln had stood there in the stand, the day would have been perfect.

19

Home Again

The Army was still encamped on the heights two days later. The evening was mild and still, and a little earlier there had been an issue of candles to the troops, meant, no doubt, for use in writing letters home. As night fell, a few soldiers stuck the candles in their rifle muzzles and lighted them. More and more men followed their example until soon the whole First Division was moving around and around like a swarm of fireflies. Carrying their candle-tipped muskets, they formed up by companies and regiments and held a huge, sparkling parade, commanded by noncoms and enlisted men. Bands struck up music, and drum and bugle corps joined in. The whole hill crest was glowing with light as they marched past the headquarters tents and saluted their generals.

It was a strangely moving sight. To watch those hardened veterans, tough as sole leather, performing such a childlike maneuver gave Ben a choking feeling. It was, he thought, a wonderful symbol of the peace they had won.

Another week passed before the Twentieth Maine left its last encampment. Even then a part of the regiment—the newer recruits—was kept in the Army. Ben's three-year enlistment hadn't expired, but since he had been through more than two years of fighting, he was given his discharge, along with Hawkes, Bean, and Preble.

They were mustered out on Sunday, the fourth of June, and the following day they marched back to Washington, led by Lieutenant Colonel Morrill. There they boarded a train for the north.

It was a muggy morning, with heat waves rising from the Potomac flats. In the day coach Ben took off his military blouse and sat back, wiping the sweat from his tanned face. Then, to his embarrassment, the regiment's commander came and sat down beside him. Morrill soon put him at his ease.

"Hot day!" He grinned. "But we'll soon be where it's cooler. Early June's a lovely time of year in Maine."

"Yes, sir," Ben agreed. "I can hardly wait to get home. I reckon the fish are biting. Colonel, I'd like it fine if you'd come up to Harmony sometime. We've got black bass that run as big as six pounds, besides perch an' a few pickerel."

"I'd like to try those bass," the officer told him with a smile. "You live on a farm, Everett?"

"That's right, sir. A pretty good farm, too. My brother's been running it all alone since I enlisted, so I guess he'll be mighty glad to have me back. Still, after the hay's in an' the corn's hoed, we generally have time to take a day off an' fish."

"What about hunting?" the colonel asked. "You're fairly close to the big woods up there, aren't you?"

"Yes, sir. Plenty o' deer an' moose an' sometimes a bear. Come fall we have about all the venison we can eat. But any time o' year we'd be proud to have you come see us."

"I'll come," Morrill promised. "Can't say when, but I'll write you first. I've heard your mother's a pretty good cook."

"The best!" Ben told him proudly. "Just let us know when, an' I'll come down to meet you at Skowhegan."

It was a long, cindery ride through Baltimore and Philadelphia and on up to New York. This time Ben didn't take the steamboat to Portland. His friends told him it would be quicker by train, so that was how they traveled. Getting home seemed the most important thing in life just then.

Used to bivouacs on the ground, Ben had no difficulty curling up in the seat of the New Haven coach and sleeping soundly. All night the cars rattled east and north, and at daylight the Maine men found themselves in Boston. There they shouldered their knapsacks and tramped across the city to the old North Station. A breakfast of fried potatoes, pie, and coffee took up the time before the Portland train was due to start.

An hour later Ben looked out of the open window of the car and knew he was really in New England. It was a tumbledown stone wall that convinced him. He had built a good many such walls, picking up the rocks, digging out the boulders, and hauling them on a wooden drag, pulled by oxen.

Behind the wall were woods—New England woods—of white pine, birch, and maple. And through a gap in the trees, somewhere north of Haverhill, he glimpsed a white-tailed buck and a doe.

In Portland they had to change cars again for the ride northeast to Augusta and Skowhegan. It was well into the afternoon by then, and that last lap of the journey seemed to stretch out endlessly. All along the way, they stopped at little stations, where farm people stood gawking. A horse would occasionally rear and snort at the terrifying noise of the locomotive. Ben chuckled. More than once he had had to hang on to old Prince when the steam cars went by.

One by one, the ex-soldiers had said good-by and left the train along the way, and north of Waterville Ben was the only one who remained. At long last the engine puffed into Skowhegan. It was then past eight in the evening, and Ben debated whether to stay at the hotel. Then he laughed at himself. Night marches were nothing new to him, and that

far north, in June, the twilight would last another two hours. He bought some doughnuts to munch along the way, shouldered his knapsack, and set off up the East Branch Road.

It had been a hot day, but now the air was cool and delightful. As the darkness gradually deepened, he could hear little night creatures stirring in the woods near the road. A fox yapped sharply and sent a distant farm dog into a frenzy of barking. Then whippoorwills began to call, and Ben whistled in answer. He was happy. Hiking along a familiar trail in comfort was pleasant work compared to some of the nightmare mud-marches he remembered.

Around midnight he left the road by the little river and cut up across a hill pasture. A moon, a little past the full, rose to light his way, and even in the pine woods beyond, he was able to keep his direction. He judged it must be close to two o'clock in the morning when he came out on the main wagon road at almost the same place where he had been cutting birches on that February day so long ago. How long? Only two years and four months, but the intervening time had been packed with so many events that it seemed like half a lifetime. One thing was sure. He wasn't a boy any longer.

Wrapping his blanket around him, he lay down on a bed of pine needles at the edge of the woods and slept peacefully for a couple of hours. The early sun, peeping over a hill to the east, shone in his eyes. He stretched his long arms, went to a nearby brook to drink and wash, then resumed his journey. At five o'clock he reached the dooryard of the home farm.

Ben knew the hour exactly because he heard a stir of movement in the house and the clank of an iron stove lid as the breakfast fire was lighted. Then the kitchen door opened, and his brother Abner came out, headed for the barn.

Abner was a big man. At the time Ben went off to war, his brother had outweighed him by forty pounds. Now they weren't so far apart in size, though the younger man might have been an inch or two taller.

"Hi, Ab!" Ben greeted him with a grin. "Don't s'pose you could use a little help with the milkin'."

Abner stood there with his eyes staring and his mouth agape. At last he pulled himself together and let out a whoop that might have been heard in the next township.

"Ben! Why, I hardly knew you! 'Tain't just the soldier clothes, either. Boy, how you've grown an' filled out! The milkin' can wait till you've seen your ma."

Mrs. Everett had undoubtedly heard the commotion, for she appeared, breathless, in the kitchen door, her arms held out. Ben reached her in two long strides and gathered her to him.

"Here I am, Ma, all safe and sound," he told her when the first long hug was over. "Now you go in an' get some breakfast started. Seem's like I haven't had a mouthful to eat in a coon's age!"

He dropped his knapsack on the step, took off his jacket, and went out to the barn with his brother. The familiar smells were all around him—hay in the loft, grain in the bins, the sweet breath of cows, and the pungent smell from the horse stalls.

"Bet you've 'most forgot how to milk!" Abner laughed, handing him a pail and a three-legged stool.

"Got to find out," Ben replied. "But I guess it's one trick you never do forget."

Soon the rhythmic drumming of jets of milk in the pails came from both ends of the tie-up. The line of cows stood chewing their cuds contentedly. No, Ben hadn't lost his touch.

The two young men talked a little as they milked—which

cows were due to freshen, how the hay crop looked, and other farm matters. But it wasn't until six o'clock, when the milk had been carried in to cool and the herd turned out to pasture, that Abner got around to asking about the war.

"It's a long, long story," said Ben thoughtfully. "Let's eat first. We'll have a lot o' time in the evenings when I can tell you some o' the things that happened."

Breakfast was on the table, and as soon as they had washed, the two brothers sat down. There were platters of fried eggs, golden-brown fried potatoes, and steaming, juicy blueberry muffins. The coffee tasted better than any Ben had drunk in the Army, and he had real cream to put in it.

"Ma," he said when he had finished, "I've been dreamin' about food like this for more'n two years. I told my tentmates you were the best cook in the State o' Maine, an' I wasn't lyin'."

He took his gear up to his old room and changed into a work shirt and overalls. Then he stood looking out the window at the green fields and the huge old elm in the yard. Everything he saw spoke to him of peace.

Some day he would be able to talk about his experiences, but for a while all he wanted to do was work, eat, sleep, and try to forget. General Sherman was supposed to have said "War is Hell." Ben agreed it was a useless waste, and there was no excuse for killing other human beings. But he wasn't sure it was all bad. He had seen acts of great bravery and generosity along with all the evil. For himself, he thought he had come out of it stronger, not only in body but in mind and heart. And the objective had been won, even at awful cost. The Union was saved.

With a good feeling all through him, he went down the stairs and out to help Abner in the barn.